15: LUCE FINDS HER HERO

"Why don't you take your things upstairs and unpack?" Mum said to Jon. "You *are* staying for a few days, aren't you?"

"Well, at least two," said Jon, getting up and looking relieved to be able to get out of the firing line.

"I expect the firm can't spare their marketing manager for more than that?" said Mum, smiling encouragingly.

"What? Oh, yes, I mean, no, I expect they can't."

He went out of the door and I noticed a puzzled look pass between Mum and Terry. How come they weren't ecstatic? They'd got what they wanted: a nice respectable son. Or had they? Something was not quite right. I felt it, and Mum and Dad obviously felt it, too.

The CAFÉ Club

15: LUCE FINDS HER HERO

Ann Bryant

Hippo

Scholastic Children's Books,
Commonwealth House, 1–19 New Oxford Street,
London WC1A 1NU, UK
a division of Scholastic Ltd
London ~ New York ~ Toronto ~ Sydney ~ Auckland

First published in the UK by Scholastic Ltd, 1998

Copyright © Ann Bryant, 1998

ISBN 0 590 19885 8

Typeset by Rowland Phototypesetting Ltd, Bury St Edmunds, Suffolk
Printed by Cox & Wyman Ltd, Reading, Berks.

Chapter 1

Hi! Lucy Edmunson at your service!

Sorry, that's just me being cynical because Jan is trying to smarten us all up. I think she must have been on an army-recruitment course or something, because she's suddenly turning rather sergeant-majorish, which doesn't suit her at all. And it certainly doesn't suit us lot. Let me explain who "us lot" are.

My five friends and I all work for Jan Geeson, who is the manageress of the local café, which is called *The Café*. Original, isn't it? Jan is Fen's aunt, and Fen is one of my five friends, so I'll start by telling you about her.

Fen is short for Fenella Brooks. Like me, she's thirteen. We're all thirteen, actually. And we all go to Cableden Comprehensive, and live in the little town of Cableden. Fen lives with her mum, her dad and her two younger sisters, Rachel, aged nine, and Emmy, aged five. Fen is thin and freckly with light-brown hair down to her shoulders. She is full of life and determination, and we call her the ambitious one.

Fen's best friend is Tash, short for Natasha Johnston. Tash is known as the peacemaker, because she's always kind and friendly. She lives with her mum, her brother Danny, aged fifteen, and her sister Peta, aged just three. Tash's hair is shorter than Fen's and much darker.

Jaimini Riva is the brainy one. This is how you pronounce her name, by the way – *Jay-m-nee Reever*. She is also my best friend. I know it seems ridiculous because I am supposed to be the crazy one, and yet I'm best friends with Jaimini, the brainy one. But that's life, and life is ridiculous.

At least mine is. Once, when I was going through a phase of thinking I was psychic, I figured that if I hung around Jaimini absolutely all the time and really concentrated hard, maybe eventually I'd start to look like her. That would be my dream. You see, Jaimini has very long, shiny black hair, beautiful big dark eyes and very dark skin. I, on the other hand, have short, frizzy reddish/blondish hair, fair freckled skin and rather boring greyish-green eyes. Quite a contrast, I think you'll agree.

It's all right for Jaimini. She's got a black father and a white mother, so she was always a dead cert for coffee-coloured skin. The other big contrast between Jaimini and me is our family set-up. I live with my mother, my stepfather, Terry, and my twin brothers Leo and Tim, aged eight. My real father lives with his new wife and their two little children, Edward and Colette. Terry has got two grown-up children from his first marriage, called James and Jon.

Leah Bryan is the musician. She plays both the violin and the piano brilliantly. It doesn't matter how often we tell her this, though, because she doesn't believe us. She thinks that anyone could do the same if they had the lessons that she's had, and if they did the same amount of practice. Leah is someone else I wouldn't mind waking up and finding myself being. You see, she's also got very long hair, only hers is fine and blonde. Her face is pale and calm and her eyes are blue. Not a freckle in sight, of course. The trouble with Leah is that she worries about everything. Even when she's got nothing to worry about she worries about that.

Andy Sorrell is Leah's best friend. Andy is the daring one. We haven't always seen eye to eye, Andy and me. While I'm gabbling on at eighty miles an hour, Andy is often quiet. It's not that she's shy or anything. Quite the opposite in fact. She just weighs things up more than I do. She even moves quietly, and we all think she's going to be a private detective or join the SAS when she's older. That's quite difficult to believe when you first see her, because she's the smallest of us all in height and build. She's got dark-brown cropped hair, quite dark skin and dark eyes. Andy lives with her mum, who's French, and her dad, who spends most of his time working in France even though he's English, and her little brother Sebastien, aged one! Andy's real name is a French one, Agnes. In French you pronounce that *Ann-yes*, which sounds nicer than Agnes, but we all stick to Andy.

So those are my friends. The thing that really unites us is that we all work at Jan's café. It was Fen who got this whole Café Club going in the first place. She wanted to earn some money and she came up with the idea of us six taking turns to work for two hours each day after school, then the sixth person working on Saturday afternoon. We have a rota so that we all get to do a Saturday – it means longer hours so more pay. We've had a few hiccoughs along the way, but basically it works very well. I'm hoping that this sergeant-major phase of Jan's turns out to be just one of those little hiccoughs, because I really don't think I can put up with it for much longer.

It was my turn to work at the café today after school, and the others were having a Coke there while I worked. I started off in the kitchen with

Kevin, the chef, who's twenty-one and gorgeous. I was just minding my own business washing up things that Kevin needed ten minutes before I'd washed them when Jan came marching in and started wiping things with a stroppy look on her face, as though she didn't think I was working hard enough. Then when she couldn't find any dry tea towels, that was apparently my fault too, because I'd put them all in the wash. I thought she'd be pleased that I'd put them in the wash as they needed washing, but she said I should have left a couple of them out because it was ridiculous not to have a single tea towel in a café kitchen. In the end I nipped out and bought one and she went absolutely spare then, saying I could deduct it from my wages because it was a waste of money when we had about nineteen perfectly good tea towels on the premises. You can't win!

Anyway, while I was in the hardware shop buying the tea towel I saw this dark-haired boy of about sixteen. He was quite ugly as it happened, but I didn't know that at first because I could only see his back view, and that wasn't ugly. He had broad shoulders and was wearing a leather jacket. The sight of that leather jacket reminded me instantly of the latest passion in my life, who is called Chris Harvey and is in year eleven at school. Obviously he doesn't even know of the existence of little me because year eights are the dust of the earth to year elevens, but I badly wanted him to notice me, and I couldn't be bothered to go about it subtly so I decided to write him a letter. I spent ages and ages working on this letter and didn't tell any of the others what I was up to, not even Jaimini.

I finished this work of art yesterday evening at eleven o'clock. Mum and Terry fondly imagined I was up in my room deep in my physics home-work, but in actual fact I'd done that by six-thirty to be sure I'd left enough time and energy to make a really good job of the letter. The end product was fantastic, but a horrible, horrible thought was occurring to me as I stared at Leather Jacket's back. I'd tucked the letter into one of my library books, and I was sure that the book was due back today. That fact on its own wasn't a problem. The problem was that Mum had got into the habit of taking library books out for her-self, too. In fact, Tim and Leo usually got their books at the same time as well, and Mum also got two or three books for Terry. That meant that on the day they were all due back, she would go round the house scooping up library books from wherever she saw them and if she didn't know who had read what, she just renewed the lot.

The question was, would she remember that I'd told her I'd finished the book with the picture of the punky-looking girl on the front cover. I'd even told her the story of what happened to the girl, Lisa. As the book was called *Lisa's Dream*, it was odds on that Mum would click on and she'd hand the book in. That meant that my beautifully composed letter to Chris Harvey would be hidden in the pages of a book on a shelf in the local library, where anyone could find it, take it home and have a good laugh at it. And that wasn't all. It meant that if it fell into the hands of the wrong person, I could find myself the laughing stock of the school.

All the way back to the café with the tea towel I imagined different people coming across the letter. In the end, I realized that apart from my five friends, the whole world was my enemy. Even if it was someone from another school it wouldn't take long to find out who Lucy Edmunson was. You could just phone every Edmunson in the telephone directory and ask to speak to Lucy. The chances of there being two Lucy Edmunsons were pretty slim, so then the person would have my address and they could make my life hell if they wanted to.

Things were looking really bad so I tried desperately to look on the bright side. Maybe Mum hadn't taken the library books back. Or maybe she'd forgotten whether I'd read the Lisa story and she'd renewed it. Or perhaps she'd found the letter, taken it out and left it on my desk. I rushed back to the café because I just *had* to know. Once inside the kitchen, I waited until Sergeant Major Jan Geeson was safely involved with the cappuccino machine, then I rang Mum.

"Hi, love. Where are you ringing from?"

"The café. Everything's fine, but I just wondered if you'd taken my library books back yet?"

I held my breath.

"Yes, don't worry. I took them back this morning."

I let out my breath and tried not to groan too loudly.

"This morning? Did you renew any of them?"

I held my breath again.

"Yes, let me see, what was it called. . . ?"

"*Lisa's Dream*?"

"No, because I knew you'd read that one. Oh dear, you didn't want to read it again, did you?"

"No it's just that— You didn't come across a letter in it, did you?"

"No, there was nothing in it, I don't think. Well, there might have been, but I certainly didn't come across anything. Was it important?"

"A bit, yeah." (Understatement of the year.) "Never mind, Mum, I'll go to the library after work."

"It closes at six on Tuesdays."

"I'll ask Jan if I can go early."

"Well, I shouldn't do that, Lucy. Look, I can pop into the library tomorrow and find your letter. I'm going right past there at ten o'clock."

"The book might have been taken out again by then."

"I would have thought the chances of that were very slim—"

"Oh, Mum, I've got to go! I'll see you later."

I rang off quickly because Jan had come back into the kitchen and was fixing me with one of her army looks – only this time I think she might have gone up a couple of ranks, because this was *scary*. She was eyeing the tea towel under my arm and instead of the expression of delight I was expecting to see on her face, there was a look of "I don't believe this".

"I thought you'd be pleased."

"Not only have you wasted time when you should have been working, you've also spent money that you had no right to spend. We don't need tea towels. We've got nineteen of the things in the wash."

"But they're wet."

"And whose fault is that?"

"Not mine. It was the fault of the person on duty yesterday because they should have seen that they were dirty and put them in the wash at the end of the afternoon. Then they would all have been dry by this morning." I was quite pleased with that speech, and I noticed a little crack in Jan's scary expression, a little chink of maybe-you've-got-a-point, Lucy.

"It was Fen on duty yesterday."

"And Mark."

There was always another person on duty with Jan, and one of us. Mark is seventeen and really nice. He's studying to be a martial-arts expert but he works part-time at the café to get some extra money.

"It's not Mark's job to see to tea towels."

"So it was Fen's fault."

"I'll have a word with her."

"Do you want me to do that?"

"No. *I* will. You take these orders through. They're beginning to pile up."

"Table three and table six," said Kevin, pointing to various plates that were ready to take through. "And table seven is on its way, so get a move on, kid."

"Don't call me kid."

I wished I hadn't said that because Kevin has got this very irritating habit of making up songs to any words that come into his head. He really appears to be deep into the song and it's not till you listen to what he's actually singing that you realize it's utter nonsense. Sure enough, as I went out with the order for table three, I could hear him singing loudly and passionately to the tune

10

of "Don't cry for me Argentina", "Don't call me kid, I'm a senior". I was tempted to put the baked spud down the back of his shirt, but I decided with great self-control to concentrate on not getting anything else wrong because I needed Jan to let me off early so I could go to the library.

As I served table three I could see Jan talking to Fen. I couldn't hear what they were saying, except that Fen sounded most indignant and she had sat up very straight in her chair. Leah and Tash on either side of her looked very concerned, and Jaimini was giving me a big frown across the café. I just ignored her. Andy was the only one not reacting, which was typical. She always weighed things up before she passed judgment and she never got into other people's arguments unless she absolutely had to.

Back in the kitchen Jan informed me that Fen had said the tea towels had not been dirty so she had left the damp ones on the rail of the Aga to dry, and those that were not quite so damp on the rack above the Aga. Jan gave me a look that suggested that I was back in the culprit's shoes. I was about to defend myself when I thought about the library and took at least three steps backwards.

"Yes, I'm sorry, Jan. It was my fault. You see, I noticed that a couple of the tea towels were looking very grubby and I stupidly thought that

11

it would be best to put them all in the wash. I can see now that that was very foolish of me and I fully take the complete and total blame for it."

"Lucy, what are you up to?" Jan asked me, narrowing her eyes. There was a glimmer of a smile on her face and I could tell she liked my speech. I don't know why she found it so amusing, though. I thought it was a very serious matter. Then I heard a noise from the Aga and, turning round, saw that Kevin was creased up with laughter. That did it for Jan, too, and the two of them clutched each other and laughed their heads off while I stood there feeling stupid and babyish, but trying not to say anything. Even though this reaction wasn't what I'd been expecting, it was better than it might have been. After all, as long as Jan was laughing and appeared to be in a good mood, there was a greater chance that she would let me off early.

Turning to the draining board I started wiping pots and pans and dishes and casseroles for all I was worth, which caused even more mirth from the Aga, but Jan had recovered and had whipped on to a tray the orders for tables five and seven, then rushed out to serve them.

I think Jan must have told Fen that I had accepted the blame because Fen gave me a very friendly wave and called out, "We're off now. See you tomorrow, Luce," as I was cutting a large slice of gâteau for a little girl with a big tummy at table four. Her tummy was going to be even bigger after the portion I'd cut her. The others all waved and Jaimini gave me a very special smile. I knew what that was all about. She was proud of me for being sensible and mature and owning up to being in the wrong. She thought I was finally becoming easier to live with. Little did she know! I would get Fen back as soon as I'd got this library book incident over with.

"Jan," I asked a few minutes later, when I'd put all my energies into acting like I was going for the Washer Upper of the Year award.

"Uh-huh?" She was slicing quiche and I could tell she wasn't concentrating. "I wonder if I could possibly leave fifteen minutes early? It's just that I've got to get to the library before it closes otherwise I'll have to pay horrendous fines, and now I've got to pay for the tea towel I won't be able to afford them, you see."

"Oh, don't worry about the tea towel. We've got a nice round twenty now, so that's good," she said unexpectedly.

"Yes, but the other thing," I rushed on, improvising madly, "is that I've got to get this book out for my history homework tonight. I won't be able to do the work without it, and old Dawson might slam me into detention, and it might be

13

on a day when I'm supposed to be working, so it really is important that I get to the library today. I thought it closed at six-thirty but Kevin says it closes at six."

"I—"

Kevin had been about to drop me in it, but had obviously decided to be kind. I didn't even realize he was listening. He's got this knack of being able to tune into people's conversations no matter how much noise is going on around him.

"Look, I'm sorry, Lucy. You really ought to get yourself organized, you know. I'm sure Mr Dawson didn't give you just one night to do the homework did he?

"He did, actually," I said. "You can ask Jaimini."

"No I can't, because Jaimini, as you well know, has gone."

"Please, Jan. Just this once. I'll even work overtime next time if you want. It really is important."

"Oh, all right," she said finally, but she was quick to add that it must never happen again.

So at a quarter to six I raced off to the library. This was cutting it fine, but I made it, red-faced and completely puffed out. The library was quite crowded considering it was about to close in a few minutes. There were three giggly girls of about ten, a couple of adults, and two or three students from Cableden Comp who were older than me and were sitting studying, looking very bleary-eyed as though they'd been hard at it since school finished. Then there was a boy of about ten, who instantly reminded me of a slightly older, slightly rougher, slightly scruffier version of my terrible twin brothers. He was staring at me, this kid, and he made his eyes cross and his head loll back a bit for my benefit. Boys! Such a waste of space, except older ones, of course. This one seemed to be in a world of his own. Weird. I just ignored him and headed straight for the teenage section, where I ran my finger along the line of M's.

My attention was suddenly distracted by the arrival of a gobstopper by my left foot. Glancing up, I saw that cross-eyes was grinning at me. I gave the gobstopper a gentle kick in his direction and instantly regretted that move, because he let out an enormous squeal.

"She trod on my gobstopper," his gravelly voice rang out as his finger pointed me out for all to see. It was a little difficult to ignore him because the librarian was clucking up to see what the fuss was about.

"She trod on my gobstopper," he repeated, in a whining tone. I gave the librarian what I hoped was the type of look an adult would have given, and softly explained that I had merely kicked it gently back to him because he had rolled it towards me.

"Hasn't this kid got a mother?" I wondered, looking round.

"We're closing in a minute, so if you've chosen your books, you should go," the librarian said to the boy. Then she went back to her desk and I went back to my M's, but the kid didn't move a muscle. He just stood there, which was most unnerving. I decided to ignore him entirely. Morris. Bryony Morris. That was the author. Now where was *Lisa's Dream*? There were two other books by Bryony Morris, but no signs of *Lisa's Dream*. I hurried over to the desk because it suddenly occurred to me that it might not have been put back on the shelf by then if Mum had only returned it that morning.

"If it's not on the shelf, it must be out," the second librarian informed me without even bothering to look up. "We're closing now," she added.

I walked out glumly and it wasn't until I'd gone about a hundred metres that I realized that the boy was behind me. I'd been aware of shuffling foot-steps, but I'd been so deep in my thoughts, trying to think exactly what I'd put in that letter, that the scuffing noise hadn't really registered in my mind properly. When I turned round, the boy said, "It's good in the library, isn't it?"

"What, rolling gobstoppers all over the carpet?" I asked him a bit sneeringly.

"No, seeing what people have left in books."

He had one hundred per cent of my attention when he said that. I shot him an accusing look: I felt sure that he knew what I was looking for, because he'd already found it himself. Yes, that was it. He wanted me to pay him, then he'd let me have it back. Nasty little cross-eyed toerag blackmailer!

"OK, hand it over!" I said, in the most seriously adult voice I could muster.

"Hand what over?"

He didn't look particularly guilty. On the other hand, he didn't look particularly innocent, either.

"My letter."

"I haven't got *your* letter," he replied, wearing that awful stubborn look that I'd seen so often on the twins' faces. "Unless it's this."

He had pulled out a piece of paper from his pocket. I snatched it from him and quickly read it. It wasn't mine. It was written on the same plain paper, but it was a message. It didn't make any sense to me at all.

Terrissed gardens. Usule place. 5 oclock. Thursday.

"Where did you find this?" I asked the boy. "And what's your name, anyway?"

"Ned. What's yours?"

I was about to say Lucy when I realized that he might still have my letter to Chris on him. "Jaimini," I replied, saying the first thing that came into my head. "So where did you find this?"

"In a book."

"Yes, but which book?"

"One about pirates or something. Or it might have been about a hospital. I can't remember."

"In the children's section."

"I think it was in the adult section. Or it might have been in the children's. I can't remember. I looked everywhere, you see."

"Why?"

"When I lived at the other place, me and my friend, we used to do it for a laugh, leave each other messages."

"And now it looks like you've found yourself a new friend."

He didn't answer. His face clouded over, and I realized something. Poor Ned hadn't found a friend at all. I reckoned he'd written that message himself and left it in a book, but nobody had found it so he'd taken it back out. I wondered how long the message had been there. This was only a hunch, but I know a bit about boys of that age because of my two brothers. The naughtier and more attention-seeking they were, the more it showed that they wanted something. That whole

gobstopper episode was some sort of cry for help,
I reckoned.

"Tell, you what," I said, on a sudden brainwave, "I can fix it for one of my brothers to leave
messages for you at the library if you want."

His whole face lit up. "Yeah!"

"Here, give me that one and I'll give it to the
twins and maybe they'll be able to meet you on
Thursday at the Terraced Gardens. How about
that?"

"Wicked!" So I was right. He handed me the
funny, badly spelt letter without hesitation. If
someone else had written the message, he would
have wanted to keep it for himself. "What are
they called, your twins?"

"Tim and Leo."

"How old are they?"

"Ten," I said, thinking that Ned wouldn't
want to exchange messages with mere eight-
year-olds.

"I've got to go now. See you, Ned."

"See you, Jaimini."

So off we both went in separate directions. As
I walked I stared at the pavement and tried to
recall exactly what I'd written in my letter to
Chris. There was no way that anyone could know
which Chris it was intended for, as all it said was
"Dear Chris". That was bad enough, though. I
wished I'd never written the stupid letter. But

Ned had got me thinking. Maybe someone would write back and leave the letter in a library book. I made a resolution to go to the library as often as I could. This could be quite interesting. Or it could be terrible. So what was new? That was pretty much how my life always went!

Chapter 2

When I got home, the twins were going mad with excitement because their half-brother, and my stepbrother, Jon, was coming home. He was due any moment. I was excited, too, but I was also pretty shocked. You see, Jon's last visit home, which was about a year ago, ended in the biggest row you could imagine between Jon and Terry. Mum had sided totally with Terry, so not only had we not seen Jon for a year, we hadn't even heard from him. He'd walked out on us, and now he was coming back. Exciting, yes, but a bit scary too, if you know what I mean.

"How come I didn't know about this?" I asked Mum indignantly.

"Nobody knew until earlier this afternoon. John phoned and just asked if he could come and stay for a few days. He's bringing someone with him but he didn't say if it was a friend or a girlfriend, or what." I was watching Mum closely, wondering how she felt about seeing her stepson again after the long silence. It was hard to tell, though she did look rather tight-lipped. "I phoned Terry at work and he's really hoping it will be a girlfriend."

"Why?" asked Leo, who has the imagination of a baked bean.

Mum hesitated at first, then said, "Because Terry's been dying for Jon to show some signs of settling down."

"What, with a girl?" asked Leo, looking disgusted.

"No, with a gorilla," Tim informed his twin, without batting an eyelid.

"I wouldn't mind settling down with a gorilla," Leo said.

"Or a baboon," Tim added, warming to the theme.

"No, not a baboon. They've got revolting bottoms."

"Well, what I mean is, *any* animal would probably be better than a girl," Tim explained.

Their conversation was mind-numbing, so I cuddled my dog, Harry, assured him I would be spending the rest of my life with *him*, and tried to get some more out of Mum about Jon.

"I can't tell you any more, Lucy. It was a very crackly line. I think he was on a mobile, and he just said he'd be arriving with someone at about six-thirty. Well, you know what Jon's like." Mum turned back to her cooking, but her shoulders moved and I knew she was sighing.

Out of all my friends' mums, mine is probably the second most laid-back after Tash's mum. And yet she really disapproves of Jon. Jon lives in London and, before the row, came to visit us about once a year if we were lucky. Terry's other son, James, is the one that Mum and Terry approve of. He's got a good job, a nice girlfriend, a small, clean flat, and he visits us about four times a year. But Jon is something else.

I remember the last time he was here, we all nearly passed out from the smell of his jeans and tatty, faded T-shirt, which he wore for three days, and probably for three years before that. I think he even slept in them. Leo had asked Jon if the reason he wasn't taking them off was because they were stuck to his body. Jon hadn't bothered to reply, and Mum and Terry had exchanged disapproving looks because they probably thought he was being rude to his half-brother. They'd seemed determined to make the list of Jon's vices as long as possible, which really bugged me, especially as I'd noticed the glimmer of a smile cross Jon's face at Leo's question.

Whenever Jon and I had been together on our

own we'd had some great times, because he's at drama college so we'd talked about acting all the time, and, of course, that's my very favourite thing in the world. Jon had made me laugh time and time again, but he'd also made me think about things, and it irritated me when Mum and Terry couldn't see that underneath the tatty clothes and the don't-care attitude there was a really brilliant person. I'd been so disappointed to find that Mum and Terry were just like so many other adults, taking everything at face value, to use a phrase of Jaimini's.

"That young man is just utterly selfish," Mum had said through clenched teeth to Terry one evening when they'd thought I'd gone to bed.

"I just despair of him," Terry had replied in a low voice.

"What can we do?" Mum had then asked, sounding desperate.

Silence had followed that question, but I could feel that it was a very heavy sort of silence. Then Terry spoke.

"Just keep on at him, I suppose, and hope that eventually it might get through his thick skull that acting's a dead-end career for all but the most determined characters." But then they'd rowed with Jon, and I'd never heard them mention him again.

All this was coming back to me now as I watched Mum getting more and more agitated. As far as I knew, Jon hadn't actually dropped out of college, which, from my point of view, was great because as I said, drama is my passion. I'm even more into it now than I was a year ago, so that made it all the more important that Jon would be here in our house very soon.

"Is Jon still at drama college?" I asked, keeping my voice ordinary-sounding.

"As far as we know, but you never can tell with Jon." Mum was looking tight-lipped again. "It turns out to be a dead-end profession for the majority of people, you know. And Jon's so disorganized, with such a couldn't-care-less attitude, that the chances of him making the grade are very slim."

I thought Mum was being rather hard on Jon, and I knew that part of the reason for that was that she was trying to steer *me* away from acting. I didn't want this speech to turn into a lecture for my benefit so I decided to get out before it did.

"I'm going to do some homework, Mum. What time are we eating?"

"Whenever they arrive."

Mum was cooking, as always. It's her job, you see, catering. It wasn't unusual to find every surface in our entire kitchen covered with dishes and pots. In fact, our kitchen looked more like a café kitchen than the real café kitchen did.

Up in my room I stared into space and imagined that Jon had turned into a famous actor and had instantly recognized my talent, told me he was going to get me an audition for a leading role in a West End musical, and that with his influence it would be no problem convincing the panel to give me the part.

I came down to earth with a bang when a picture of Jon, looking as though he'd never had a wash in his life and sounding as though he wouldn't be able to learn a single line to *save* his life, came into my mind. Now I was thinking in the same way that Mum and Terry had been. I must stop it. Jon had always been my hero and that was not going to change now. I decided to think about something else, and this made me go straight back to the incident in the library.

"Right," I told myself, "I must sit down and try to remember exactly what was in my letter to Chris." So I got out a sheet of paper and tried to rewrite it. The more I thought about it, the more stupid and embarrassing it sounded. I was going bright red just thinking about it. If only Mum hadn't taken that book back to the library. Anyway, this is how it went, as far as I can remember.

Dear Chris,

    I really badly want to talk to you, though half of me doesn't know how to put into words all that I feel. [God, how yuk-making. I bet whoever read the letter would have a really good laugh. Either that or be sick.] If you agree to talk to me, can you give me a sign? Anything will do. I know I'm only thirteen and you're in year eleven, but I'm very mature for my age. Please don't breathe a word of this to anyone.

That was more or less it, as far as I could remember. I looked at it written down, and in a flash I realized something. I hadn't actually signed it. I definitely hadn't, because at the last minute, when it was all done, I'd hesitated over whether to suggest a meeting place, and I'd decided to think it over during the day. So this wasn't too bad, after all. Nobody could accuse me of writing this letter. I hadn't left a single clue in it. After all, there were loads of thirteen-year-old girls around. It could have been any one of them. I heaved a big sigh of relief. Then I sat down on my bed and flopped backwards in horror because I'd forgotten about the two biggest clues of all. The letter was in my handwriting, but worse than that, like a fool, I'd written it on the back of a letter from school about the charges for school dinners and,

27

of course, that meant that the school's name and address were there for all to see.

I thought about this problem for a few minutes and eventually decided that it would still be possible to deny all knowledge of the letter. I could say that someone had done an amazing job of imitating my handwriting. The very next day I would change my style of writing, and make sure that everybody knew that I didn't write in the old style any more, so if ever the letter did come to light, I could say I didn't even write like that any more.

"They're here!" came a wild shout from downstairs, and I leapt up and went to my window, all thoughts of letters and handwriting leaving my head instantly.

At first, I thought that Tim must have been wrong, and that this was someone else arriving, because the car was far too clean to be Jon's. For his last visit home, he'd arrived in a beaten up old car with loads of rust all over it and the exhaust pipe hanging down. The car that was pulling up now was white and gleaming. What's more, it was a Ford Fiesta, which wasn't at all the kind of image that Jon liked to project.

Keeping back, I watched with great interest as someone got out of the driver's side. After a few seconds I came to the conclusion that, by pure coincidence, someone else happened to have turned up at the very time we were expecting Jon, because this person was certainly the same age, but was neat and tidy, with smart clothes. I kept an eye on the passenger door, expecting that at any moment the friend would get out, but the door didn't even open, and the man was walking up our drive. He glanced up and I jumped out of sight, then I belted downstairs, bursting with curiosity. I was already composing the story I was going to tell the others the next day. I just knew I'd have them gripped. I practically fell through the door into the kitchen to find Mum brushing some broken crockery into a dustpan. Poor old Mum. She really had worked herself into a state. I bet she was dying for Terry to get back from work.

She started massaging hand cream into her hands and forearms, which is what she always does after she's been cooking, only this time, it looked like she'd poured half the bottle out and was having great trouble rubbing it in.

It had been a year since I'd see Jon, but as I'd had a sneak preview from my bedroom window, I knew that he looked totally different from the last time. I also knew that Mum would probably faint with the shock unless I warned her.

"I just saw Jon getting out of the car, Mum. I think you'll be pleased. He's all smart and clean."

"Oh—" Mum didn't have time to say more

than that because there was a light knock at the door, then in he came, gently calling, "Hello". Even my warning hadn't prepared Mum for the shock of the transformation. She was clutching the worktop behind her. I didn't know where the twins had got to. Maybe the sight of this new half-brother had been all too much for them and they'd crept off without a word.

"Well, it's lovely to see you," Mum stammered. "A lovely surprise! Yes."

Poor Mum was really rattled, and no wonder. It wasn't only the clothes, you see. Jon's hair had been a lot longer than mine when I'd last seen him, and it had looked as though it would have been impossible to get a comb through it. Mine is tangly enough, but I'd had the idea that Jon's was proving a home for a fair few bugs!

"You look . . . well. . ."

I thought Mum was about to say that he looked like someone else, but she must have decided that it wouldn't have been very polite. So far, Jon hadn't said a word. He'd just looked round the kitchen as though savouring the joy of being home. It was all so weird. Without any warning, he suddenly went over to Mum and gave her a kiss, then he turned to me.

"This can't be little Lucy!"

I smiled nervously. What was it with this guy?

Why did he make me nervous? I was *never* nervous, for goodness' sake. He kissed me on the cheek and he smelt of aftershave. His skin felt smooth. I just couldn't get over the massive change in him. I mean, his trousers had creases in them. He was wearing a crisp, pale blue shirt neatly tucked into them. His shoes were proper shoes, not trainers, and they looked as though they'd been cleaned that day. I stared at him, expecting him to say something about the last time we'd seen him – the fateful day of the massive row and the beginning of the long silence. When he spoke, though, it was just a simple fact he came out with.

"The effect of the job," he said, with a sort of sheepish smile. My spirits took a dive because if he'd got a job, that meant he wasn't at drama college any more. I knew I should have felt pleased for him, and for Mum and Terry, because their drop-out son had apparently turned into the type of person they really approved of, but I couldn't help feeling hacked off that my castle in the air had fallen down.

Jon grinned round at us. Then he spotted the twins, who had been hiding from him, but had obviously been too gobsmacked or curious to stay hidden, and had crept out from behind the pantry door. They stood there on their spindly legs, moving from foot to foot and looking extremely embarrassed to see their brand-new half-brother in this changed state.

"Hi, you two!" said Jon. "Still identical. Still impossible to identify!"

He was smiling and looking totally relaxed, but somehow it wasn't wearing off on us because we were all too stunned. Mum was the first to recover.

"Come and sit down. Let's have a cup of tea, or maybe we should have a proper drink. We must celebrate your job, Jon!"

"Yes, whatever. That would be really nice," Jon said. "Where's Dad?"

"He should be back any minute. Come and sit down you lot." This was to me and the twins, because we were standing around looking gormless. I did as I was told immediately, but the twins looked at each other and wrinkled their noses.

"Can we watch telly?" asked Leo.

"Well, that's not very welcoming to poor Jon," said Mum.

"No, don't worry about me," smiled Jon. "I'll catch up with those two scallywags later. I'm sure they'd rather watch television than listen to a load of boring adults' talk."

I rose in my seat. He was classifying me as an adult! The twins couldn't get out fast enough. Mum was fussing round the kettle and the teapot, so I leaned my elbows on the table, cupped my chin in my hands and gave my stepbrother the benefit of my most mature and interested expression.

"Are you alone, Jon?" I enquired, feeling like a counsellor for a moment.

"Sorry?" He looked a bit confused, but then understood what I was getting at. "Oh, you mean, where's Kirsty? Well, she should be here tomorrow. She sends her apologies for not making it at the same time as me, but she got rather tied up with work, you see."

I caught Mum smiling into the tea packet, and as I knew she wasn't *that* fond of tea leaves, I took it that she was pleased that the missing person was a female. I was right.

"Oh, a girlfriend! Lovely."

"Well, not exactly, more of. . ." Jon trailed off, suddenly overcome with embarrassment. Mum frowned and spilled a few tea leaves off the spoon on their way to the teapot. She liked to have things in nice, neat compartments. She wanted Jon to give a few facts and figures about this mysterious Kirsty person so she could get it straight in her mind.

"And what's this job you've got then, Jon?" Mum continued, trying to resume normal service. "Last time we saw you, you were. . ."

Whoops! Mum had got it wrong again. She was going red.

"Dossing about. Yes, I know," Jon finished Mum's sentence for her. Surely he would mention the row they'd had, but if he *was* going to he didn't get the chance because Mum was talking again.

"Well, I wasn't going to say that exactly," she said with a nervous laugh. She was lying, though. I could always tell when Mum was telling porky pies because she looked down and started doing unnecessary things. Like right now: she was stirring the boiling water round and round in the teapot. Fair enough, stir it a little, but this was big, violent stirring.

"I think it's probably ready to pour now, Mum, isn't it?" I said.

"Yes. Yes, of course. Oh, look, here's Terry. Hello, love. Look who's here!"

Poor old Mum was acting like a battery-operated toy that someone had forgotten to switch off. She was so relieved to see Terry coming into the kitchen. I think she was glad to have the spotlight off her at last. I couldn't work out why Jon was making her so nervous. It was true that he was almost like a stranger, but I thought adults were supposed to be able to cope with these things. Here was Mum, though, acting like, well, like me.

"Hi, Dad!"

"What the. . . ! This isn't my son, is it?" Terry

let out a great roar of a laugh and rushed forward to shake Jon's hand and give him a big bear hug.

"'Fraid so," laughed Jon.

They were grinning away at each other and Mum was watching them with her head on one side and a fond smile on her face. I realized I must have been staring, so I quickly changed my expression to a nice big beam to match everyone else's, then Terry sat down and the conversation got more relaxed. How typical of Terry to be so open and friendly right from the word go. I expect some dads would have waded in with a big telling-off all about walking out without a word and never getting in touch, but not Terry. He's so fair like that.

"Come on, then. Tell us all about it." Terry got straight down to basics.

"What do you want to know first?" asked Jon.

"What you're doing, or who you're seeing, or whatever it is that's brought about this transformation."

"I think it's a bit of both, really. I've got a job as marketing manager for a fruit-and-vegetable packaging firm, and I've met Kirsty."

"Great news! Marketing manager? That was a bit sudden, wasn't it?"

Great news? Huh! I thought it was the worst news of the century. I didn't want a marketing manager for a brother. I wanted the actor back.

At that point the phone rang and Jon jumped out of his seat. It was Jaimini wanting a chant, but I was so into the conversation round our kitchen table that for once I didn't feel like chatting. I took the phone into the hall and sat on the bottom stair, where I very quickly and quietly filled Jaimini in on my stepbrother, his awful new image, the mysterious Kirsty, Mum's reaction, and the fact that he'd dropped out of drama college and got a job that sounded really boring. Jaimini listened with a few gasps, and just one comment:

"This Kirsty person must be a very strong character to have transformed your stepbrother like that."

"Yeah, well, there are strong characters and strong characters, Jaimes."

"What do you mean?"

"I mean I have the horrible feeling that I'm not going to like this particular strong character if she's changed my highly original brother into a follow-the-crowd-and-have-a-safe-job type of guy. But it's weird because when Mum mentioned the word 'girlfriend', Jon started stammering about how she wasn't *exactly* his girlfriend. I can't work it out. Although he did say that the new job had also helped with the transformation."

"Well, it might be the job, but I doubt it. I

was once watching this programme on telly with Mum, and there was a bloke who smartened up in that, and Mum said it would turn out to be a woman who'd been responsible for the transformation. Well, she was right, and when I asked Mum how she'd known that, she said that when a man went through a complete change it was nearly always due to a woman's influence."

"Look, I've got to go, Jaimes, because I want to hear what they're all talking about. I'll tell you everything tomorrow."

"OK, see you then."

So we rang off and I rushed back into the kitchen to find the adults running out of conversation. This was the very last thing I'd expected to happen. It was really weird. I decided to give them a helping hand.

"So, what do you have to do in your job, Jon? Is it difficult? Did you have to learn all about it incredibly quickly? I mean, when exactly did you decide to leave college? I was hoping you'd still be there. . ."

"Dear me, don't bombard the poor man with questions!" laughed Mum.

Jon, meanwhile, looked distinctly uncomfortable.

"But I want to know," I persisted.

"All in good time," said Terry. "I think I'll have a glass of wine. What about you, Jon?" He was trying to sound relaxed, but somehow, it didn't really ring true.

"Yes. That would be great."

Now, I'm no psychologist, but Jon was definitely hesitating there. My mind started working overtime. Maybe he'd turned into an alcoholic and he knew he shouldn't be drinking, but he'd decided to risk it so that his family wouldn't wonder why he'd given up.

"Who was that on the phone, Lucy?"

Now this was really scraping the barrel. Mum had never been interested in my phone calls until this moment in time. She must have been desperately short of conversation. I'd had enough of this. OK, so Jon didn't want to be bombarded with questions, but surely just one wouldn't cause any harm.

"It was Jaimini," I answered, then I turned to my stepbrother. "Did you drop out of drama college or were you chucked out, Jon?"

He did a double take, then recovered.

"Well, I decided to call it a day. I guess I finally came round to realizing that it might turn out to be a dead-end road."

"But you were so committed," I said, feeling pleased with the word "committed" but also feeling cross with Jon for being so wimpy. Mum and Terry might have been happy about the great change and the wonderful return of the prodigal son, but I certainly wasn't. I'd thought Jon had more guts than this. Before, I used to boast about having a stepbrother in the acting profession, and I liked his scruffy image, but now he was just like any other boring adult with a nice safe life. I was beginning to go right off him.

"Why don't you take your things upstairs and unpack?" Mum said to Jon. "You *are* staying for a few days, aren't you?"

"Well, at least two," said Jon, getting up and looking relieved to be able to get out of the firing line.

"I expect the firm can't spare their marketing manager for more than that?" said Mum, smiling encouragingly.

"What? Oh, yes, I mean, no, I expect they can't."

He went out of the door and I noticed a puzzled look pass between Mum and Terry. How come they weren't ecstatic? They'd got what they wanted: a nice respectable son. Or had they? Something was not quite right. I felt it, and Mum and Dad obviously felt it, too.

Chapter 3

The following day at morning break, the six of us went down to the netball courts, which is our favourite outdoor meeting place. Nobody ever goes down there during break times, so we are always guaranteed privacy. Goodness knows what old Hawkeye, the science teacher, had been on about for a whole double period. I certainly didn't have a clue because my mind had been on more important things. I'd come up with a really great idea.

I couldn't stop thinking about what that boy, Ned, had said about how he'd had a sort of library pen-pal. It struck me that it would be a fantastic thing to do, and I'd decided to do it myself. I was pretty convinced that whatever Ned had said, he'd actually taken my letter to Chris, so that was the end of that. Even if he hadn't taken it, and someone else had, I'd decided not to worry too much. Besides, I had my new scheme.

Some gut instinct made me decide not to tell the others about my latest idea. I could just imagine Jaimini warning me that it was dangerous because you never knew who you could be writing to: they might turn out to be a mass-murderer or something. No, this was going to be my secret. All the same, I couldn't wait to share with the others my news about the spruced-up Jon.

"Go on then, Luce," said Fen. "We know you're dying to tell us something. Spill the beans."

"How do you know that?" I asked her indignantly.

"Because you're acting like you're sitting on a bomb," Jaimini told me.

"Well. . ."

They all leaned forwards. I love telling stories. I do have this habit of exaggerating rather, but in this case there wouldn't be any need to exaggerate. The real thing was interesting enough.

"Well, Jaimini knows about this already, but my stepbrother, Jon, turned up out of the blue yesterday evening."

"Just like that?" asked Leah.

"Well, he phoned Mum in the afternoon and said he would be arriving at about six-thirty, and that someone would be with him. You remember what he was like the last time he showed up at our place? About a year ago?"

"Really scruffy."

"Yeah, well, you should see him now. He's hardly recognizable. He's neat and clean and respectable. It makes me sick. Just because Mum and Terry went mad at him the last time he came home and told him off for being such a slob, Jon's changed everything. But the real downer is that he's only gone and packed up drama college!" I paused for effect, and when I'd clocked that everyone looked suitably hacked off on my behalf, I continued. "Now he's got a proper job as a marketing manager for some firm or other. It would have been great if I could have discussed acting with him, although, to be perfectly honest, I can't imagine myself discussing anything with him. He's too, sort of, nice. I used to really rate my brother and now he's just boring. It's all right for Mum and Dad. They've got what they wanted, but what about poor me? My good-fun brother has disappeared for good and I do *not* like the replacement. The twins didn't know what to make of it at all."

"What about the friend?" asked Tash.

"She never arrived, and frankly I don't care. If she's behind the big change in Jon, then I hope I never meet her. She must have taken over his mind as well as his wardrobe. I just wish Mum and Terry had left poor Jon alone in the first place. He can't even choose his girlfriends properly now, poor brainwashed thing."

"What are you on about, Luce? You're just overreacting," Jaimini said in her most teacherish voice.

"I am *not* overreacting."

"Well, the poor girlfriend doesn't really stand a chance, does she?" said Fen. "You've decided that she's a wicked witch with evil powers, and you haven't even met her."

"I'm not saying that," I said, only just managing not to shout, because my friends were being very thick about what I was trying to explain. "I'm saying that Jon is now a boring person, so if it was his girlfriend who's caused that, then she must be boring, too – with flat shoes, a pleated skirt, a tight perm and a job as a librarian. Anyway, we don't even know if she *is* his girlfriend. Her name's Kirsty, but Jon went all weird when Mum asked him about her. You know, he started stuttering as though Mum had pressed a button marked 'Please Start Stuttering Now'."

"You're mad, Luce," said Jaimini, but she was laughing.

"I think it's very intriguing," Tash said.

"What do you think, Andy?" I asked her, half of me dreading the answer.

"Same as Tash," she replied, which made me

feel very happy because Andy's opinion somehow counts the most, if you know what I mean.

"Try and think of something more you can tell us about Jon," said Leah, leaning forwards.

"I don't know what to make of him. He even seemed to hesitate before he said yes to a glass of wine. Can you imagine? My stepbrother, whose room was so littered with lager cans after his last stay that they kept turning up in peculiar places weeks after he'd gone."

"When are we going to meet this new Jon, then?" asked Fen.

"Do you want to?" The others all nodded and seemed really enthusiastic, and I felt quite flattered that they were that interested. "Well, I could always invite him to come down to the café with me."

"Brilliant idea, Luce," said Leah warmly. "Why don't you go and give him a ring now?"

So at the end of break I rang home from school, but Mum said that Jon had gone out. "The spare room is so tidy, Lucy. I can't wait to meet this Kirsty. Her influence must be amazing."

"Do you think Jon might be back before the end of school? Only we were wondering if he wanted to come down to the café to see where I work."

"He didn't say when he'd be back but I'll pass on your message as soon as he gets in."

When we were sitting in the café later, I kept on wondering if Jon might suddenly turn up. Every time the door opened I had to look to see who was coming in, but as time went on I realized he wouldn't be coming.

"Ask him to come tomorrow, then," suggested Tash.

"Maybe Kirsty'll be here by then, and she could come too," said Jaimini.

The café was quite crowded and Fen was rushed off her feet. I was glad it wasn't me on duty because whenever there are loads of people around to watch me, something always goes wrong.

"Shall we play our guessing game?" suggested Leah.

This is a game that we often play. We pick a customer, or more than one if we feel like it, and we imagine as much as we can about them, such as how old they are, what their name is, what their job is, etc etc. The frustrating thing about this game is that I always want to go up to the person afterwards and find out which one of us has come closest with our guesses. Once or twice, Jaimini has had to stop me from doing just that. It always surprises me that Andy doesn't dare to go up to people and ask them outright, but she says it has nothing to do with daring, it is to do with being mature and tactful. Fen says it's also to do with keeping your job. And it is true that if ever Jan found out that we'd been going up to complete strangers and asking them personal questions about themselves, she'd probably sack us on the spot. I can't help being impulsive, though. That's just the way I am.

"What about her?" Leah asked out of the corner of her mouth.

"Who?" I asked, craning round to see who she meant, because she wasn't giving us any clues at all.

"Don't make it so obvious, Luce," hissed Jaimini, so I repeated my question without moving a muscle, which made Tash crease up.

"Don't look now, but the lady at the table nearest the door to the kitchen."

I was dying to look but I made myself study my plate, which was totally clean except for the stone from the middle of the olive that had been on my slice of pizza. Normally we don't eat anything in the café, just have a drink, but today, probably owing to a mind-blowingly boring afternoon watching an ancient video in the hall as it was too wet for games, we were all starving and also reckoned we deserved a treat. We ordered a large pizza between the five of us and wolfed it down in about fifteen seconds flat. I don't know if it was because I was concentrating so hard on not looking at the lady that Leah was talking about, but I suddenly found myself filled with the irresistible urge to flick the olive stone as far as it would go. If I flicked it straight ahead it would go in between Jaimini and Andy and would land on the floor, then I could go and pick it up and nobody would be any the wiser, but I would still have had the satisfaction of flicking it. Before anyone could try and talk me out of it, I took aim and flicked. Hard!

Unfortunately, the lady at the closest table, behind Jaimini and Andy, chose that moment to bend down and pick up her napkin, which had floated down just behind her. I watched in horror as my olive stone hit her on the cheek.

"Ow!" she shrieked. "Who did that?"

The others all knew it had been me, but they didn't want to get involved. I kind of hoped that if I kept quiet this whole situation might just go away, but Tash was nudging me with the back of her hand on the side of my knee, and Jaimini's foot was jabbing my leg under the table. Andy's eyes were boring a hole in my head and Leah was going pink and telling me out of the corner of her mouth to "apologize quickly".

"Sorry, I didn't realize it would hit anyone. I didn't think it would go that far, you see."

At that point Jan arrived on the scene. Wouldn't you just know it! I sometimes think Jan has got a special set of antennae specially designed for catching me out if I dare to put a single foot, or finger in this case, wrong.

"Is everything all right?" she asked, cautiously smiling at the lady whose cheek I had stung with my FOS (Flying Olive Stone).

"No, everything is not all right, actually. You seem to have a group of delinquent teenagers in here. One of them has just deliberately fired an olive stone at me. It was very painful, actually."

I saw Andy's eyes narrowing and knew that I had to take the blame – and quickly.

"It was nothing to do with the others, Jan. It was entirely my fault. I just couldn't resist flicking my olive stone, but I never thought it would go that far, and anyway, I wasn't to know that she was going to bend down at that moment, was I?"

"I am sorry, madam," Jan said, turning her back on me, having heard all she wanted to hear. She bent over and we could hear her trying to smooth things over, inviting her to have another drink on the house and that kind of thing.

"You idiot, Luce," Jaimini said softly, but when I looked up I saw that she was having a job not laughing, as were all the others, even Andy, who had been positively smouldering about twenty seconds earlier.

I let out a giggle and so did Tash, and in the end we were all in agony because of the effort of having hysterics but not being allowed to let it out. Tears of laughter were brimming in Jaimini's big eyes, and Leah's cheeks had got more colour in them than I think I'd ever seen. We were still in this state when Jan turned to us a minute later.

"And as for you, Lucy," she began, but even she had seen the funny side of it, and she just shook her head and walked away, trying to hide her smile. I let out a sigh of relief. The woman left the café a few minutes later and the moment she'd gone, we all cracked up. Then I suddenly remembered something important.

"I think I'll get going, actually," I said, "because Kirsty might have arrived and I can't wait to see what she's like."

So I left the others, but I didn't go straight home because my reason for going was not to see Kirsty. It was because I wanted to get my first message planted in a book in the library. At lunch time, when Leah was at orchestra practice, Andy and Fen were at cross-country club and Jaimini was helping Tash with her geography, I nipped off to the IT room where it took me less than five minutes to print out the following message:

I am a thirteen-year-old girl, interested in most things except school. If you read this and want to reply, put your message in a book by any author beginning with D. Check the date stamp to make sure it's not a popular book and sign yourself LF. My code name is SF.

That was all I wrote because it made it more fun not knowing at all who the other person was. I felt really excited as I rushed off to the library. I love adventures, and the more secretive, the better. LF stands for Luce's Friend and SF stands for Stranger's Friend, because that was what I would be – a friend to a complete stranger.

Inside the library I checked that there was nobody around that I knew, then I went to the teenage section and tried to find the most popular book I could, because I wanted to be sure that my letter wouldn't be sitting embedded in a book for months on end. I think the most thrilling bit of this whole thing was that my "library-book friend" and I would have to keep our wits about us to make sure that nobody else intercepted our letters. This first message had to go into a popular book, but after that we had to choose only books by unpopular authors. It was all so exciting. In the end I chose a book by my favourite author and left my message folded over and tucked right inside the pages roughly halfway through, then I put the book back on the shelf and left the library.

Most of the way back I hugged my secret to myself, then as home drew nearer and nearer, I began to think about Kirsty and to wonder what she'd be like. Now I'd pictured her in flat shoes with a pleated skirt and a tight perm, I couldn't think of her any differently, I could only add to the picture, so I added tortoiseshell glasses, no make-up, a string of pearls and a neat brown cardigan. She made me sick!

Pushing open the kitchen door I wanted to call out, "Is she here? What's she like?" but I made myself keep quiet in case she was sitting at the kitchen table sipping tea with Mum. Sipping tea was one of the things I could imagine Kirsty doing quite a lot. And I bet she was always poring over a book, but it wouldn't be an exciting novel, it would be someone's biography, someone that nobody had ever heard of. And Kirsty wouldn't sprawl in an armchair or flop on her bed to read, she'd sit at the kitchen table, sipping her tea. She really *did* make me sick.

My eyes scanned the kitchen quickly. Nobody was in there so I went through to the hall and called out to Mum. No reply. I called out to the twins. No reply. I then called out to Jon. No reply. So I went back into the kitchen and found a note on the table. "Popped over to Mrs Stone's with twins."

Mrs Stone is a nice old neighbour of ours who's got two pet rats that used to be mine. That's another story! I felt really disappointed that nobody was around, but only for a moment, because I quickly remembered that it was still only quite early and Kirsty might turn up any time. As I was thinking that, the door opened and in walked Jon.

"Hi, Lucy. Good day at school?"

"Not bad. I was wondering, do you want to come down to the café with me one day? I work there once a week. Me and my friends take turns, you see. They'd love to see you again. I've been talking about you."

"I wish I'd been a fly on the wall for that conversation! Hope you only said nice things."

Goodness knows why, but I found myself blushing. "I was . . . just . . . telling them what you're like now, and everything."

"I bet you were telling them how much I've changed."

"Yes, I did mention that," I admitted.

"Tell me, Lucy, do you think I'm completely different, or do you think there's still some of the old me lurking around?"

The question was quite a difficult one to answer, because to tell the truth, I didn't think there was any of the old Jon still "lurking around" as he put it, but I got the impression that this wasn't what he wanted to hear, so I said, "You're still the same underneath. You're just neater, because of the new job, I guess. Only I wish—"

I stopped abruptly because, let's face it, I

couldn't really say, "I wish you weren't so boring", could I?

"You wish what?" he prompted me.

"I wish, er, I wish I could meet Kirsty," I
finished.

I wasn't mistaken, Jon definitely blushed a bit
when I said that. So I was right. He was ashamed
of her with her neat, tidy appearance and her
sensible shoes. It must have been that. In the past
Jon's girlfriends were always just like him – tatty
jeans, pierced noses, that sort of thing. I could
just imagine them, and I bet they had tons more
character than boring Kirsty.

"Is Kirsty here yet?" I continued.

"No, not yet," he replied.

"So when *is* she coming? Soon?"

"Er, unfortunately she can't come today. . ."

"Oh." The frustration must have shown on
my face. I was dying to see if I was right about
what she was like. I wanted to ask Jon why she
wasn't coming, but decided that might be rather
nosy. "Is she coming tomorrow, then?"

"Yes, hopefully."

Mum and the twins came in then, and Mum
immediately got down to the great British subject
of tea.

"A nice cup of tea," said Mum. "That's what
I need. Poor old Mrs Stone offered me tea about
fifty times, but never quite got round to putting

the kettle on. She's so obsessed with her pet rats that she forgets about us mere mortals."

"Pet rats!" said Jon, and for a while everyone had rat mania and talked loudly about the antics of Zinc and Zonc, which were the names of my old rats. Then Terry came in and did more or less what I'd done earlier on: glanced round the kitchen immediately to see if the new girlfriend had arrived and what she looked like.

"No Kirsty?" he asked.

"You're as bad as the rest of us," said Mum, kissing him. Then she turned to Jon. "You see, Jon, we're all dying to meet your friend."

"Yeah, cos me and Tim have been having bets about what she's like. We've got it all written down, and one of us might turn out to be very rich when we see her," Leo informed us all brightly.

"I can't believe this," said Jon. "What sort of thing have you written down?"

"What her hair's like."

"What her clothes are like."

"Yeah, and if she's fat or thin or tall or small or whatever."

"And . . . other stuff, too." At this point, Tim let out a typical eight-year-old-boy giggle, and Leo immediately did the same.

"I think that's enough of that conversation," Mum warned them, aiming a sharp frown at them both. They gave one more token giggle then rushed out.

"I can't describe her, really," Jon said. "You'll have to wait and see."

"I'm sure she's lovely," said Mum, giving Jon a reassuring look. She felt sorry for him, it was obvious, but I wasn't quite sure why.

As I lay in bed that night I had plenty to think about. First I tried to imagine what my library friend would look like. My favourite picture of her was that she looked very much like me, and when we finally met up with each other we wouldn't believe how similar we were. Maybe she'd be quite thick like me, too, but good at acting. And perhaps we'd get together and make a video and send it to a film company – or wherever you're supposed to send things like that to – and they'd snap us up as the latest sensation for the millennium. It would be fantastic!

I realized I was getting rather carried away, but it was lovely having all that happiness in store. And if it turned out to be someone I didn't like it didn't really matter. I'd soon know from the type of message she left me, and I'd simply not bother to reply if I thought we weren't going to get on. My eyes were closing but they flew open again as I remembered the other message that had got into the pages of a book by mistake. I shook that horrible thought out of my head and tried to think of something else. Kirsty. That's who I would concentrate on. Mind you, *that* was a pretty horrible thought, too. All the same, I went over my mental picture of her, then I thought about what Jon had said. Why was he being so cagey about her? Maybe it was more than I'd thought. Maybe it wasn't just that she was neat and ordinary and boring. Perhaps she was very ugly, or far too old, or even far too young for Jon.

At that point in my thoughts I must have fallen asleep. All I know is that I dreamt that Kirsty was a kangaroo. That was the unusual thing about her. In my dream I was absolutely appalled about Jon going out with a kangaroo, but nobody else thought there was anything wrong with it and Mum thought I was being really prejudiced in my attitude. When I woke up in a sweat in the middle of the night, I could still hear Mum saying to me, "Lucy, I'm shocked! I'd never got you down as kangarooist!"

Chapter 4

First period on Thursday I have French with Leah, Fen and Tash. At the beginning of the lesson I scrabbled about in my bag for my French book but I couldn't find it anywhere.

"We didn't hand our books in on Tuesday, did we?" I asked Leah.

"No. I never take mine out of my bag from Tuesday to Thursday usually. That's funny. . ."

"What?"

"I can't find mine, either."

"I can't find my book anywhere," hissed Tash from across the aisle.

"We must have handed them in and forgotten about it," Leah said. She turned round to the boys on the desk behind. "Did we hand in our books last time?"

"Dunno," said one of them. He'd got this really dopey expression on his face, and I realized he wasn't the best person in the world to ask about missing French books because he was always losing everything. Anyway, he was too gobsmacked about being asked something by the beautiful Leah Bryan to be able to do anything but stare. Poor, sad boy. I turned to the boys on the table on the other side of me but the question never left my lips because I could see their books on their desks. Looking round, though, it looked as though all the girls were searching for their books.

"What's all this noise?" asked Mr Farmer, the French teacher. He's not one of the strictest teachers, but he isn't at the other end of the scale, either. Just average, really. "Come on, get yourselves organized. Let's make a start."

"We can't find our books, sir," Fen informed him.

"Oh, right. You didn't hand them in last time, did you?"

"No, we definitely didn't," a girl called Marie told him. Mr Farmer likes Marie because she sits at the front and always pays attention.

"I've got mine," said Mark Wilkinson.

"Yeah, me too," said another boy.

It turned out that I was right. More than half of the girls' books were missing, but none of the boys' were.

"Something's going on, sir, because my maths

book was missing this morning," said one of the other girls.

"Yeah, and I couldn't find my geography book anywhere," added another.

Mr Farmer was looking exasperated. I knew that look. He was cross with himself because he couldn't find an obvious solution and he was at a loss as to what to say. There was a knock at the door at that moment.

"Come in."

It was a boy from year eleven. I didn't know his name, but I *did* know that he was a friend of Chris Harvey, and my stomach turned over. I just knew that this little visit was going to have something to do with me. He was carrying a pile of exercise books.

"I've got some French books here, sir. For some unknown reason they turned up in our form room. It was, er, Chris Harvey who found them, but he asked me if I'd return them."

I could feel myself tensing up at the sound of his name.

"Oh, excellent timing!" smiled Mr Farmer. "There you are, girls. All is well again. Thank you, Luke."

"What about my maths book? I don't suppose that turned up in your form room, did it?"

"Er, I don't know about any other books."

And that was the moment that I realized what

all this was about. My stomach turned over. The reason the girls' books had been taken and not the boys' was because Chris Harvey wanted to check all our handwriting. I could feel a blush creeping up under my freckles. I wondered if Luke knew which of us was Lucy Edmunson, because by now it was obvious that he knew it was Lucy Edmunson who had written the message. I wanted to die. Luke dumped the books on Mr Farmer's desk and took a final look around the room. I kept my head down until I heard the door click shut, but thought afterwards that that was probably the biggest giveaway. I could just imagine him reporting back to all his mates, with Chris Harvey in the middle of them: "You should see your great admirer, Chris. Poor you! She's got red hair and freckles." I closed my eyes slowly and heaved a big sigh. Why wasn't I born pretty like Leah? Life was so unfair.

"Are you all right, Luce?" Tash asked me, leaning over and touching my hand with hers. She's so kind and nice.

"Yeah, fine." I nodded vigorously, going with my gut instinct. If there was to be any chance at all of my coming out of this stupid situation without losing too much street cred, I would have to keep up the pretence that I'd never sent the message in the first place and that someone had imitated my handwriting. That meant that right from the word go, I mustn't show that I was worried. I had to act completely normally. Fortunately, the one thing I *am* any good at is acting. I'd completely forgotten about changing my handwriting style, though, and thought I'd better not start now, because that would be too much of a coincidence. It would point the finger at me more than ever.

At break time, the six of us made our way down to the netball courts and I reported to the others the conversation I'd had with Jon and what I'd been thinking about Kirsty. I could see Jaimini smirking to herself when I said I thought Kirsty might turn out to be either really ugly or really ancient.

"Why do you always assume that whatever I think must be rubbish?" I finally demanded, flashing my eyes at the whole lot of them for good measure.

"We don't think it's rubbish," Jaimini answered. "We just know how much you like the drama of things like this, so you may be blowing things out of proportion, that's all."

I was about to have another go at them when I realized the others weren't even looking at me. Their eyes were on someone approaching us across the field. I couldn't tell at first if it was a student or a teacher, then, as the figure drew closer, I realized it was someone from year eleven.

"Who's this coming?" asked Andy.

"It's that Luke boy, isn't it?" Fen answered.

"Who's he?" asked Jaimini, who wasn't in our French group.

"He brought a load of the girls' French books back for us," explained Leah, as Luke drew even nearer and I felt more and more sick. "Apparently they turned up in the year-eleven form room. Goodness knows why."

"Well, I wish my history book would turn up in the year-eleven form room," said Jaimini.

"Yeah, *and* my English book," said Andy.

"This is really weird," said Fen. "Something's definitely going on, you know. Hang on a sec."

"What?" asked Tash.

"He's got more books with him."

By this time Luke was almost up to us. With every fibre in my body I wanted to look down, but I made myself look up with a normal, inquisitive expression on my face, just like the others wore.

"Is one of you lot called Jaimini Riva?" he asked.

"*Jay-m-nee*," we all corrected him, because he'd pronounced it wrongly.

"Is that my history book?" asked Jaimini. "And how come all our books have gone missing all of a sudden, anyway?" she added, quite indignantly for Jaimini.

"Dunno. They just keep turning up in our

form room. Anyway, which one's Agnès Sorrell?"

"*Ann-yes*," Leah corrected him, using the French pronunciation.

"Andy," said Andy quietly. Then she turned her big, probing eyes on him. "What's going on, Luke?"

It was the fact that she'd used his name and was speaking so quietly, with that intense gaze of hers, that made him look suddenly very uncomfortable. Next she stood up, which made him take a step back. I wished I was as scary as that. It was ridiculous. Andy is the smallest of us all, and yet here she was intimidating a year-eleven boy!

"Is one of you lot Lucy Edmunson?" Luke then asked, which made my stomach yo-yo. The others turned to me, and I tried with all the concentration I could muster to pretend I was on a stage and was acting the part of a girl who had nothing at all to feel guilty or embarrassed about. "It's you, is it?" Luke then asked, following the eyes of the others and visibly relaxing. I swallowed and gave him my most casual stare, even though my heart was beating much faster than usual and my mouth was beginning to feel dry at the thought of what he might say next.

"I've already got my French book back," I said, in the most "normal" voice of the century.

"I know," he replied, with a knowing look that

I ignored. Then he turned to Andy. "If you want to know what's going on, ask *her*." He jerked his head in my direction, then off he went.

There was a brief silence while all eyes followed Luke's disappearing back, then one by one they turned to me.

"Well?" asked Andy.

There was something about the tone of her voice, all teachery and accusing, that really got to me.

"Well, don't look at me! How should *I* know what's going on?"

"But why did he think you *did*?" Jaimini asked me. *Her* tone of voice irritated me, too. I'd heard it so often before. She was getting all revved up for a Let's-get-at-Luce session. She'd already had one of those this morning, over me being too dramatic. I could feel myself getting wound up.

"Look, I really don't know what he's on about, OK!" I said, in a raised, cross voice. "So just leave me alone," I added for good measure.

"We were only asking," Jaimini said defending herself. I liked that – the royal "we". She was deliberately bringing the others into her little camp, and leaving me on the outside. It made me sick the way they ganged up with each other against me. Well, I could do without Jaimini more than she could do without me. *She* hadn't got a library friend, had she?

"I'm going," I said in a disgusted voice as I got up and brushed the gravelly bits off my trousers.

"Where?" asked Tash, the only one who really cared, probably. It was a pity that she'd been the one to ask me that because I didn't want to snap back at Tash.

"Dunno," I replied gruffly as I walked off.

"Oh Luce, come back, please," I heard Jaimini say, when I was about twenty metres away.

I didn't even bother to answer. I was glad that she felt guilty. The only thing that was worrying me was whether or not I'd slightly overdone my act. I mean, it wasn't really an act – I had genuinely felt cross, but it was only because they were getting so close to finding out how I was involved in Luke's book-stealing operation.

"Now, calm down, Luce," I told myself sternly as I walked back towards school. "Think carefully. Don't act on impulse." It seemed to me that as long as I didn't do anything silly, this whole thing would blow over. Luke had had his bit of fun. He'd found out who Lucy Edmunson was, and that was that.

It was no good. I wasn't convincing myself. Luke might have had his bit of fun, but Chris Harvey hadn't, had he? This was probably only the beginning. Oh, no! I carried on walking with my eyes on the ground and a frown on my face, and a couple of minutes later I found myself standing in front of my locker. Something told me that I ought to take a good look in my French book. I'd been writing in it during the lesson, but I hadn't examined it thoroughly. Maybe there was something in it. I opened my locker and rummaged around, then stopped abruptly as I realized that I'd handed my French book in. We all had, at the end of the lesson, because Mr Farmer wanted to check the work that we'd done that morning. It suddenly became very important that I get hold of my book, and break was almost over. I rushed to the staffroom and asked for Mr Farmer. He appeared almost immediately.

"Could I possibly have my French book back for a minute, please, sir? I think I—" I had been about to say "left something in it," but Mr Farmer didn't seem interested in my world-shatteringly important reason for wanting my book back. He returned to the door in about ten seconds flat with the book in his hand.

"As long as I have it back by the end of the day, Lucy," he said with a nod, then he turned away and started talking with another member of staff. I'd obviously interrupted an important conversation. That was why he hadn't been interested in me or my explanation. Good – the less my behaviour was spotlighted, the better.

I shut myself in a loo, turned my French book

66

upside down and shook it vigorously. Nothing came floating out of it. But I had to be sure so I opened the front cover, preparing to go through the book page by page. There was no need. A very thin piece of paper lay between the cover and the first page. It had got wedged right into the seam of the book. I removed it with trembling hands and read it.

Dear Lucy,

You didn't sign your message, but my detectives have been working hard and it didn't take them long to work out who my thirteen-year-old admirer is. Meet me by the old oak tree (such a romantic place, don't you think?) at lunch time today and we can talk. This letter is my sign, by the way. Hope you think it's subtle enough. I haven't breathed a word to anyone, don't worry.

Chris.

If my hands had been trembling before, they were positively shaking by the time I'd finished reading the message. It was all one huge joke to Chris and his friends. They'd obviously sat round together and composed the letter to make me look as big a fool as possible. As for saying that he'd not breathed a word to anyone, that was the biggest insult of all. And all that stuff about the old oak tree. I didn't even think there *was* an oak tree on our school premises. Before, I had felt uncomfortable, embarrassed, guilty and worried, but now all I could feel was very angry, and equally determined to pay Chris Harvey and his mates back. I also wished I could pay back whoever had given him the message. How had it fallen into Chris's hands so quickly? I know there'd been a huge clue that it must have been someone at Cableden Comp because of the letter being written on the back of a school note, but all the same, it had found its way to Chris Harvey amazingly quickly. I sat on the toilet lid puzzling about this.

A thought suddenly struck me. If the book went out immediately, the library might know who had taken it out. It could have been someone who had specially requested it as soon as it came in. I'd once specially requested a book and the library had notified me the moment that it had come in. I *had* to find out. I looked at my watch. The bell was about to go. And so was I!

But first, I would hand the French book in. I would leave the letter tucked in it, only a little more obviously than it had been before. I carefully placed it between the front cover and the first page. Only this time I deliberately left a little bit sticking out at the top of the book. I wanted

Mr Farmer to read it. I had decided to call Chris Harvey's bluff. With any luck this would kill two birds with one stone. I intended to pretend I'd never even received the letter, which would take all the fun out of the joke as far as Chris and his friends were concerned. Then there was always the chance that Mr Farmer might ask to see me and show me the letter.

"Do you know anything about this, Lucy?" he would ask me in a serious voice.

I would frown as I read it, then turn to him with a baffled look on my face, and say, "I haven't a clue what this is about. I don't even know anyone called Chris, so I'd hardly be likely to be getting letters from them, would I? I think this message must be meant for someone else, sir."

Yes, that would be good. That would be mega. But first I had to find out who had taken the book out, and I couldn't wait till the end of school to do just that. I looked at my watch. The bell would be going in about a minute. I had to hurry. I rushed to the staffroom and asked the teacher who answered my knock if she would give the book to Mr Farmer. Then I headed for the gap-in-the-hedge exit, which is the best way to get out of the school without being seen. Fortunately, the bell went when I was almost there, so with all the toings and froings going on at that time I didn't think anyone would possibly spot a little year-eight girl disappearing from the premises.

Once safely outside, I shot off in the direction of the library. The library isn't far from school, but I'm not fit like Andy and there was no way I could run all the way. Then I spotted an ice-cream van. I knew I mustn't stop and buy an ice cream because that would just be drawing attention to myself, which was the very last thing I wanted to do. I didn't want anyone reporting me for skiving. All the same I was starving, and the ice creams looked really tempting. There was a queue of three people so I wouldn't have to wait long. It wasn't that I was in a tearing hurry, but I thought that I ought to get back to school for afternoon registration, otherwise questions would be asked, and if I was going back for the afternoon, then I would need something to eat.

I wasn't absolutely sure how to treat the others. I didn't think it would be wise to say that I'd left the premises. I'd pretend I'd simply skipped a couple of lessons because of feeling so angry and upset with them all. Then they'd all be very apologetic and sorry for me, and if anyone from year eleven made any suggestions that I fancied Chris Harvey, my friends would all defend me like mad, which was what I wanted.

The queue was down to the one woman in

front of me, and me. The trouble was that this woman turned out to be just one of a party of hikers. They'd all got rucksacks on their backs, and every single one of them wanted an ice cream. It was taking ages and ages. What made it even more frustrating was that they were all so chatty. The ice-cream man was wasting tons of time because he kept stopping what he was doing so that he could join in the conversation, like he couldn't manage to do two things at once. Then on top of that, the lady in front of me suddenly started chatting away, and when she turned round and saw that it was me and not her friend Ethel, she nearly killed herself laughing and kept patting my arm and saying, "What a cuffuffle, dear!"

I didn't know what on earth a cuffuffle was, but I couldn't help liking her because she was so smiley, and in the end I found myself telling her all about myself, and the others started tuning in and chatting too, as though I was their best friend.

When my turn finally came, I got my cornet and handed over my money. I didn't rush off immediately as I'd planned, but instead had a conversation with one of the other hikers, who was called Betts, all about dog training. In the middle of this I suddenly realized that I ought to make a move, so I wound up the conversation really quickly, turned round far too suddenly and walked slap-bang into a lamppost. "Ouch!" I squealed, clutching my forehead, which sent my ice cream catapulting all over the windscreen of a car that was parked right by me.

"Oh dear, are you all right?" asked Betts, as a few of the others came fussing round me. It had been rather a painful experience, but I wasn't in agony. In fact, I was more concerned about how on earth to get the enormous dollop of chocolate ice cream off the windscreen of the parked car before its owner came back.

Too late. A lady was walking briskly, head down, in our direction, and I just knew that she was going to turn out to be the owner of the ice-cream-drenched car. It was tempting to root in Bett's rucksack, take out the first thing I came to, even if it was a pair of knickers, and start vigorously rubbing away at the ice cream, but I knew I hadn't got time, because— *Omigod!* Guess who the owner of the vehicle was? The olive-stone victim!

Chapter 5

At first she didn't pay any attention to the group of people standing beside her car. She was obviously deep in thought and she simply unlocked the door and got into the driver's seat. Through the little brown streams of chocolate ice cream that were sliding slowly down the windscreen, I could see the shocked expression on her face. Then our eyes met, and if expressions had voices, hers would have said, "I might have guessed it would be you!"

As she was getting out of her car and I was preparing to face the music, the hikers were still going on about my little argument with the lamppost.

"Do you think we ought to call an ambulance, Moll?"

"What do you think, dear? What *is* your name, by the way?"

"Lucy," I mumbled.

"And how do you feel, Lucy? You're looking very pale, dear."

I assured them I was absolutely fine and thanked them for their concern, then, timing it to perfection, making sure that Mrs Olive Stone definitely heard me, I said, "I'm only looking pale because I've got a lot on my mind, you see."

This very adult statement went down a bundle with the hikers, who made loads of sympathetic noises and nodded wisely to each other. In fact, they were so impressed that one of them scampered off to tell the rest of the bunch, who were still chatting up the ice-cream man, and the next thing I knew, they were all standing round nodding and smiling at me, presumably to see if there were any more pearls of wisdom on their way out of my mouth.

Mrs Olive Stone was not to be taken in quite so easily, however.

"I take it I'm indebted to you, Lucy, for this piece of art work?" She'd remembered my name. Not good. "And shouldn't you be in school?"

We were on very dangerous ground here. I thought I ought to get off it as fast as possible. Maybe a joke? As usual, I didn't think. I just said the first thing that came into my head. Giving her a nice smile, followed by a sort of nervous giggle, I said, "Oh well, that's two to me!"

This went down like a lead balloon. Her eyes widened and turned thundery.

"I do not see this as a game," she said.

Oh, why wasn't she a sweet, innocent, sympathetic older lady, like the lovely hikers?

"Yes, I know, and I'm really sorry. If you've got a tissue I'll wipe it off. I banged into the lamppost, you see, because I wasn't concentrating. Well, I was, only I was concentrating on something else, you see." While I'd been talking, I'd managed to find a couple of crumpled tissues up my sleeve and I'd started trying to clean up the windscreen, but I seemed to be making it worse.

"Leave it, leave it. I'll do it," said Mrs Olive Stone, somewhat impatiently as she got back in her car, pressed a button that started spraying water in great jets on to the windscreen, then set the windscreen wipers going at their fastest speed. This was much more efficient than my crumpled tissue technique, I can tell you, and I was just thinking of making a getaway while things were starting to improve when the windscreen wipers stopped abruptly and out got Mrs Olive Stone.

"So, what are you doing out of school, Lucy?"

Like magic, an excuse found its way into my head and out of my mouth with wonderful timing. "I've just been to an appointment at the orthodontist with my mum, and she dropped me off at the library to get a book I need for school. She'll be back to pick me up in a minute, so I'd better go and get my book."

"Oh, your mother's coming to pick you up, is she? In that case I might stay and meet her," said Mrs Olive Stone, to my horror.

"I think we'll be pushing on then, dear. Now we know you're in safe hands. Goodbye."

"Thank you very much indeed for looking after me," I said gratefully to Moll and Betts and the others, then I waved to them all as off they went, smiling. As I was waving brightly, my mind was doing cartwheels because I had to get rid of Mrs Olive Stone, and pronto.

"Actually, Mrs. . . ?"

"Wickham. Miss."

"Actually, Miss Wickham, I only said that my mum was coming back to pick me up because I thought you, or those nice ladies, might have worried about me and felt that you ought to stay with me, and I didn't want to waste anyone's time, because, as you can see, I'm perfectly all right. Mum did drop me off here, but she had to go, and she left me to make my own way back to school, because it's only nearby."

"Well, perhaps *I* should give you a lift."

"That's very kind of you, but I might be ages in the library."

"I don't mind waiting."

"No really, I love walking."

"Hm. Well, if you're sure you're all right?"

"Yes, I'm perfectly sure, Miss Wickham."

I gave her my best smile and said a silent prayer of thanks as she got into her car and drove off. Then I raced the last few metres to the library and only slowed down at the door, so that my entrance wouldn't attract anyone's attention. I headed straight for the teenage section, and ran my finger along the books by authors beginning with D. Then I went back to the first one, took it off the shelf, and flipped through the pages quickly. Just to be sure, I turned the book upside down and shook it gently. I repeated this with every single book by every author beginning with D. There was no note.

Then something struck me. I hadn't checked whether my note had been taken or not. I scanned the shelf where the book with my note had been, then I scanned the shelf above and the one below. Then I studied all three really carefully. The book was not there. It had been taken out. Three cheers! I now had a library friend. All I had to do was to wait for her message.

Right, on to the second and most important part of my reason for coming to the library. I approached the counter, preparing a sentence.

"Excuse me, but do you know the book *Lisa's Dream* by Bryony Morris?"

"Not intimately, no, but I know *of* that book," said the librarian with a false smile. I can't stand grown-ups who try to be clever like that. I was tempted to be rude, but decided that that wouldn't help me get the information I wanted.

"Well, can you tell me who's got it out, please, because I think I left something tucked between the pages by mistake, and I want to see if I can get it back."

"Our system may be clever, but it's not that clever, I'm afraid," said Miss Cocky. I managed with great difficulty to keep up my nice warm smile.

"I did come and look for the book the same day my mum brought it back, and it had gone already, so I wondered whether it was someone who had specially requested it?"

"Probably. Yes."

"So does that make a difference? I mean, have you got it on the computer if someone specially requested it?"

"No."

Well, thank you very much, Miss Incredibly Helpful.

I thought she was giving me a rather peculiar look as I turned and went out of the library. I was feeling pretty downcast, especially at the thought that I now had to face my friends. Or did I? It seemed to be a much nicer idea to go home. I could tell Mum that I'd been sent home because I wasn't feeling well. No, that was no good, because someone would have rung Mum from school and asked her to come and collect me. On the other hand, I really wasn't feeling well. The top of my nose was throbbing like mad. I put my hand up to touch it and got a shock because it didn't feel right. It was all swollen. I must have given it quite a bang. I needed to get to a mirror. There was one in the library.

I slipped back inside and looked at myself in the mirror. Oh, dear. The bridge was so swollen that I looked like a boxer. Fortunately, it wasn't black or yellow, but I had the horrible feeling that that was coming next. Now there was no way I could go home or back to school. Of the two, though, home seemed a better idea. I would sneak in and put some frozen peas on it. I'd seen Mum doing that on Leo's hand when he had a swelling once. Let's pray she wouldn't be at home.

I did not enjoy that walk home one little bit. I kept thinking that at any second I'd see someone I knew who'd get straight on to the phone to school and report me for skiving. It was a great relief when I turned into our road. Now for hurdle number two. Please let Mum and Jon be out! Unfortunately, I could see from quite far away that Jon's car was there, but as I got nearer

I noticed that Mum's, on the other hand, was not. Maybe it didn't matter about Jon. Could I trust him? I knew he was my stepbrother, but that somehow didn't make matters any easier. All the same, I'd *have* to trust him because it was unlikely I'd be able to get in the house, help myself to frozen peas and something to eat, then get out again without being seen.

The back door was open so I went in. All was quiet. I tiptoed through to the hall and thought I could hear talking coming from upstairs. There wasn't a television in any of the upstairs bedrooms, but there might have been a radio. I wasn't sure. I stood on the bottom stair and listened. It didn't sound like a radio. It sounded like Jon's voice, though I couldn't be absolutely sure. I strained my ears for the sound of another voice, then I definitely heard Jon say, "I'm just working round to it." I held my breath and stayed as still as a statue. If Jon was talking, there had to be someone else in his room. For the second time I thought his girlfriend, Kirsty, must have arrived already, but for some reason or other, she didn't want to be seen.

This was ridiculous. I was beginning to feel like an intruder in my own house, but I couldn't resist creeping up a few more steps to have a better listen. Unfortunately, clumsy idiot that I am, my hand dislodged a vase that sits on the little windowsill halfway up the stairs. The vase rolled and thumped down a couple of stairs, then got wedged against the bannister.

"Oh hi, Lucy! It's you. I thought we'd got a burglar. What are you doing home?"

He had appeared at the top of the stairs faster than you could say "frozen peas".

"Well, it's quite a long story."

"That's OK, I've got plenty of time. I was just beginning to feel bored as it happens. Come on, let's go and get a snack. I'm starving." He had come down the stairs and spotted my nose. "Lucy! You haven't been in a fight, have you?"

He looked genuinely concerned. His arm steered my stiff body into the kitchen, and it was he who went to the freezer and came back with the frozen peas. "Here, slap these on to help the swelling. What happened?"

"I don't want Mum to see me here."

"No, she won't be back for ages."

"How do you know?"

"Because I checked."

He stopped and we both looked at each other. So he had checked, had he? There really was something going on. It sounded like Jon had more to be secretive about than I had. I was beginning to wonder if we could trade secrets. That would be good.

"I thought I heard you talking when I came in, Jon," I began, without looking at him. There was a pause before he replied.

"I've got an important report to write for work. I was speaking into the tape recorder, to get my ideas sorted. It's much better for me to work in a peaceful atmosphere. That's why I was checking when your mum would be back."

Loads of thoughts passed through my head. My gut feeling was that he was lying, but then I changed my mind, because it was a perfectly reasonable explanation. After all, why shouldn't he be writing a business report, and why not talk into a tape recorder? I felt very guilty for having had suspicious thoughts about my stepbrother.

"And now *I'm* back, giving you grief," I said, with a sorry-about-that smile.

"You're not giving me grief, Lucy. Tell me what happened to you, anyway."

"My friends were getting on my nerves, so I decided to get out for a while."

He was looking at me as though I'd just told him I'd burnt down the school. "What? Just like that?"

It did sound rather dramatic, but there was no way I was going to tell him about writing to Chris Harvey and being sussed, as well as trying to get myself a library friend and all that. It sounded so juvenile. He'd wonder why on earth his dad had got involved with a woman with such a pathetic example of the human species for a daughter.

"It's slightly more complicated than that, but I don't want to go on about it really."

"That's OK. As long as nobody's been duffing you up!"

"No, nothing like that."

We sat in silence for a moment, then I found that I was getting soaked by the drips coming off the rapidly defrosting peas, so I jumped up to investigate how my swelling was getting on. Jon still didn't know how I'd got it in the first place. It was nice of him not to press me into telling him.

"This café of yours, Lucy. . ."

"Yes."

"I wouldn't mind coming along and having a look at it later."

"Oh yes, that'd be good. My friends are all dying to see you again."

"Are these the same friends who were getting on your nerves?"

I'd forgotten about that. "Yes. Maybe today wouldn't be a very good time, after all. Can you come tomorrow, Jon?" I was trying to think who would be on duty. I thought it would be Tash today, and Jaimini tomorrow.

"You remember Jaimini, don't you?"

"Yes, course I do. How could I forget your best friend? And what was that little one called? Andy! That's right. I remember how she argued with me about politics. She was really impressive. Then there was that musical girl. Now what was her name? Don't tell me . . . Leah! They're all so interesting, your friends. You're really lucky, you know."

He trailed off looking really sad all of a sudden, and I felt sorry for him.

"Aren't your friends interesting, Jon?"

"Well, yes, I suppose so. I think my old college friends are more interesting than my new ones."

"I couldn't believe it when you said you'd left college, Jon," I said very carefully. "And now I really can't believe it, because you seem so depressed about it."

"Well, it's different. You can't go on chasing a dream, can you?"

"What was the dream? Becoming a famous actor?"

"Just becoming an actor. You look at things differently when you've got . . . you know . . . responsibilities."

"What responsibilities?"

"Well, you know, *things*."

I didn't have a clue what he was on about, but I felt horrible going on and on about it, almost as though I was rubbing it in that he wasn't any fun any more. And all the time at the back of my mind, I was thinking, *I bet it's Kirsty who's made you like this, all boring and safe and full of talk of responsibilities.* Because I wanted to bring a bit of life back to poor Jon, I said, "Actually, Jon, do come to the café today. I'm just being silly about my friends. It was a stupid argument. It'll be over by the end of school."

"Maybe I'll come along then," he said, then he suddenly gave me a big grin. "I've not completely changed, you know, Luce."

I wanted him to carry on so perhaps I could understand him more, but I made the mistake of plonking my glass down on the table, which somehow broke the spell.

I then said I thought I ought to be getting back to school before anyone missed me.

"I'll give you a lift."

"Are you sure?"

"Course I'm sure. What are stepbrothers for? Let's have a look at you."

He put a finger under my chin and examined the top of my nose closely. "It really works, doesn't it, the frozen-pea treatment?"

I looked in the mirror. The swelling hadn't disappeared, but it had certainly gone down a lot. "Yeah, you're right."

Ten minutes later I was entering the school premises, feeling like a burglar. Somehow, slipping out of school is easier than slipping back in. I decided that I'd better act completely confident and normal. After all, if someone spotted me acting furtively they'd start asking questions, whereas the sight of a year-eight girl walking round as though she was simply coming back from a dentist's appointment didn't warrant a second glance. So I sauntered in.

As I was sauntering, I was also working out how to play it with my friends. I was trying to decide whether they'd be cross with me for going off in a temper, or worried about me because I'd disappeared, or what. I came to the conclusion that it didn't really matter either way. I would surprise them all by apologizing.

Yes, that was it. I'd say that Luke What's-his-name had been talking rubbish when he'd told Andy to ask me what was going on about the missing exercise books, because I hadn't a clue what he meant. Then I'd say that I was only mad with them because I was frustrated that, as usual, nobody seemed to take my thoughts seriously, and I was really worried about my stepbrother. I wouldn't say anything about the library, naturally. I'd just say that I'd gone home because I wanted to talk to Jon. Then I'd tell them about overhearing him. That would intrigue Andy. And you only had to get Andy interested and all the others automatically followed suit.

It was right in the middle of lunch, so it was the perfect time to arrive at school. The moment I was on the premises I simply blended into the general rabble. I wondered whether the others would be down on the netball courts, and was about to make my way down there when I was nearly flattened by Andy charging at me. She can move so fast.

"Where did you spring from?" I asked her.

"I could ask you the same question," she replied. I couldn't tell from her expression whether she was cross or worried. I wished one of the others would show up. My wish was granted. Fen arrived on the scene.

"Where've you been?"

"Home."

"Home!"

Then the others came up to me.

"We were really worried about you," said Leah. "We've been keeping watch from the window." She *did* look worried, but then Leah always looks worried.

"What did you go home for?" asked Jaimini. "Honestly, Luce, you really exasperate me at times."

This was better. This was more how Mum would have reacted. Jaimini was only letting her crossness show through because she'd obviously been really worried.

"Let's go down to the netball courts and I'll tell you all about it," I said, trying to sound just a little mysterious. We were halfway down there when I realized I was absolutely starving and my packed lunch was in my school bag in my locker. I decided to go and get it. "I won't be a sec. See you all down there," I said.

So I ran off to my locker, but as I was rounding a corner in the corridor, my passage was stopped by four year-eleven boys. One of them was Luke.

"Not so fast, Lucy Edmunson," he said with a snigger.

"I'm trying to get my packed lunch," I told him, feeling irritated because I can't stand it when boys start acting cool and cocky. They think they're so big and clever. They'd never act tough if they were on their own. They always had to be in a group.

"Can you move, please?" I asked, still keeping my tone quite hard. I was beginning to feel a little shaky because the boys had spread themselves out to make it quite clear that there was no way they were going to let me through. They didn't look threatening or anything, but I felt such a fool because I was powerless to move.

"Quite subtle for a year-eight kid, aren't you?" another of the boys said to me. When I looked at him he was grinning like a Cheshire cat, and being me, I immediately went pink.

"I don't know what you're talking about," I replied as lightly as I could, because I couldn't think of anything else to say.

"Oh, that's rich, isn't it, lads?" said a third boy, looking at the others and sniggering. That made them all snigger, of course. These boys were getting seriously on my nerves and I knew at that moment that I had two choices. Either I admitted the whole thing, let them have a good laugh, and asked them nicely to leave me alone from now on if I promised never to disturb their friend Chris again, or otherwise I had to continue to deny the whole thing, and pretend I really didn't know what on earth they were on about. I only had about a microsecond to decide which option to go for, and I went for the second. Right, come on Luce, act! Don't let them see you're rattled or they'll only tease you even more.

"Look, what is all this about? Why am I being cornered in a corridor by four big thugs? Do you want me to yell the place down or something? I'm perfectly capable of bringing the entire staffroom down here in about three seconds flat, you know. Want to see me in action?"

That was good. Correction. That was brilliant. I didn't know where that speech came from. I think I must have taken a leaf out of Andy's book. Talking of leaves in books, I wondered whether that was the reason for all this. Maybe Mr Farmer had found that note in my French book and told Chris off for teasing a poor, innocent year-eight girl, which was what I'd hoped would happen when I'd left it in there. The trouble was that I wasn't supposed even to have seen the note, because I didn't know anything about anything. I had to keep remembering that, otherwise they'd suss me instantly.

"How come you think I know anything about missing exercise books, Luke? I don't get you, I really don't."

"Don't play the innocent with us, little Lucy Edmunson," replied one of the others.

"I'm not playing the innocent. I don't know what you're talking about, and I'm very hungry, so will you please move before I scream."

I'd tried my best to be forceful and strong-sounding, but they were still standing about, grinning and sniggering.

"Fine. Go and get your sandwiches."

The four boys stood to one side with a bow, as though I was the Queen. I tried to hold my head up and walk normally, but I could hear that they hadn't gone away. Goodness knows why I was letting a bunch of pathetic boys worry me but my heart was definitely beating more loudly than usual as I unfastened my locker and took my sandwiches from my bag.

"Got any more love letters in there?" said one

of the boys, which instantly sent the others into peals of laughter.

"I don't write love letters," I said, sounding as impatient as I could, and keeping my back to them all while pretending to look for something else in the locker. I didn't think my red face went properly with my hostile voice.

"Oh, come on, you must think we're stupid."

"Yep," I said, which took a lot of courage, I can tell you.

"We've checked out the handwriting and it's definitely yours. And wasn't it a piece of luck that your sweet little message found its way to lover boy so quickly, eh?"

I was using every ounce of mental energy I possessed not to react, even though I was dying to know who it was that had taken out the library book. I started eating one of my sandwiches and kept rolling my eyes to the ceiling as though I was having to put up with a gang of six-year-olds. Then a mild drumming noise started somewhere in the corridor. It took me a few seconds to realize that raindrops were hitting the window pane quite forcefully. It must have been raining hard. That meant that everyone who was outside would come rushing in. Good. The sooner the better. I was still munching away and they were still standing there trying to look threatening. I was beginning to feel more and more angry at the frustration of not being able to get away from their taunts and jibes. For about the tenth time I wished I'd never ever written that stupid letter.

"Making very heavy weather of that sandwich," said Luke.

"Yeah, it's making me hungry," said one of the others.

"Here, let me have a bit," another one of them chimed in, and I'm sure they would have nicked one of my sandwiches if Andy hadn't appeared at that moment, or, to be accurate, Leah appeared first, then Tash, but both stopped in their tracks when they saw the year-eleven boys. Andy took in the situation at a glance and kept walking, while the other two hung back, along with Jaimini and Fen.

"Are they bothering you, Luce?" said Andy, in her normal voice.

When she spoke, the four boys just fell about laughing. It wasn't a real laugh, of course. It was a nasty, sneering laugh.

"Who's this? Superwoman's daughter?" said the boy with the deepest voice.

"I hope they haven't nicked your sandwiches, Luce?" Andy went on, ignoring the boys as though they were flies.

"Shall I go and get a teacher?" Leah called.

"I shouldn't bother, Lee. There'll be one along any second now, and they'll take one look at this little scene and have these louts for the very worst sort of bullying."

"But we weren't bullying," Luke protested, sounding pathetic all of a sudden.

"Oh, no?" said Andy, looking at him as though he was a silly little boy whom she despised but also felt sorry for. Then she turned to me and spoke sarcastically for the benefit of the boys.

"Stop looking so perky, Luce. I know they're only a bunch of pathetic-looking boys who couldn't scare a fly even if they took a degree in fly-scaring, but all the same, I think it looks better for any teacher who might happen to appear if you try to seem a *bit* scared. Hey, what's that on your nose? It's all swollen!" She was peering at me. "Did one of this lot do that to you, Luce?"

I was shaking my head but she was ignoring me.

"Oh dear, dear, dear," she went on, turning to Deep Voice and looking him in the eye, while imitating the most motherly type of teacher. "Looks like these big boys are in even bigger trouble, doesn't it?"

The boys had begun to look rather uncomfortable, as though they were desperately trying to seem disgusted but not quite succeeding. In fact, with Andy's last words, their eyes had started darting about in alarm, as though they were weighing up the odds of a teacher appearing. At that moment the bell rang.

"We never touched her!" protested Luke in his whining voice.

"Tut, tut!" said Andy, shaking her head slowly.

"Come on," said Deep Voice. "We'd better get going. I've had enough of this pathetic bunch of girls."

"That's right, chickens," Andy threw after them as they scampered away. "You run along like good little boys."

"Andy!" hissed Leah as the others approached. "Stop it. They'll make you pay for that."

"Yes, please be careful, Andy," said Tash.

"Thanks, Andy," I whispered, feeling my whole body starting to tremble, like a sort of after-effect.

"*Did* they hit you?" she asked.

"No, it's OK."

"Thank goodness for that. Otherwise I would have reported them."

"No, it was a lamppost that hit me."

"A lamppost!" squealed Jaimini, as the others all gasped. "Look, can we talk, Luce?"

"But the bell's gone," Leah pointed out.

"Are you coming down to the café after school?"

"Yes, and Jon might be coming."

"Who's on duty?"

"Me," said Tash, "but Fen can fill me in later."

"Let's meet at the gap in the hedge at the end of school and we'll all walk down together," said Fen.

So that was agreed.

Chapter 6

Afternoon school was not good. As we changed lessons I walked down the corridor looking over my shoulder or staring at the floor, expecting that any moment I'd fall down a man hole, or catch my foot in a booby trap. I knew I was getting paranoid but Andy really had gone for the jugular, and I hated to think what would happen now. One thing was certain. Chris Harvey's mates wouldn't just let it rest.

During history I sat at the back and went over all that had happened that day. One thing that was puzzling me was why Chris Harvey himself hadn't once appeared. How come it was Luke What's-his-name gunning for me all the time? The memory of him and the rest of his nasty species made my blood boil. I knew they were only taking the mickey and having a laugh, but in a way Andy was right. It was a sort of bullying.

Maybe the others would have some ideas? I'd already decided that, embarrassing though I knew it would be, I'd have to explain the whole Chris Harvey thing to my friends. Apart from anything, it wouldn't be fair of me to keep Andy in the dark when she'd got me out of such a scary situation with those year-eleven thugs. So yet again, I wished I'd never *ever* written that stupid lovesick letter to Chris. I'd dramatically changed my view of him since I'd met his charming friends. With friends like that he must be a pretty horrible person himself. Trust me to fall for such a nasty piece of work. Goodness knows what I ever saw in him anyway!

I definitely wasn't going to mention anything about my library friend to the others, just stick to what had happened to make those four boys confront me like that. It was quite a relief knowing that in about an hour's time I would have unburdened myself of all that, and I would also have talked through my thoughts about Jon. Actually, I wasn't so much thinking about Jon any more as about Kirsty. I was sure she was a problem. And maybe that was just my usual overactive imagination that everyone was always going on about. In a way it was tempting to turn the Jon and Kirsty thing into a big drama to draw the attention away from my childish behaviour over Chris. I knew I would come in for some stick from the others about writing that letter, but really it wasn't my fault because I'd never meant to leave it in a library book, after all.

In the end we decided to wait till we were all sitting comfortably at the café before I started on all my news because it was impossible for everyone to hear me while we were walking along. Fen said that she felt really sorry for Tash because she had to work, but Tash assured us all she didn't mind, and said she'd look forward to hearing my news later. So when we got to the café, Tash went in through the back door to the kitchen, which is what whoever of us is on duty always does. The rest of us went in through the front door and were greeted by Becky, who is the other part-timer who works in the café when Mark isn't on duty. Becky is in her early twenties, but acts like she's about fifty. I don't know what it is about her. It's not that I don't like her, just that I've got nothing in common with her. She even makes my mum seem young and trendy, she's so old-fashioned.

"Nice to see you, girls," was her opening line, delivered with a big smile. Big smiles and pleasant opening lines were not Becky's usual style, so of course I immediately felt guilty for having eyed up her very recently, very tightly permed hair as we'd come through the door, thinking it reminded me of a poodle stuck on top of her head.

"Oh, Becky, you're not usually that pleased to see us," I couldn't help saying, while Jaimini dug me in the ribs, which felt like a gentle tap. (I'm immune to Jaimini's rib-digging activities.)

"I'm *not* that pleased to see you," Becky replied, "it's just that if you lot are here, Tash must be here too, and I'll be pleased to see a bit of help in this place, I can tell you."

Well, that got me back, but it wasn't like Becky to be quite so openly hacked off. I looked round for Jan. We all did, as we sat down at a table for five.

"Over there, talking with that lady. Has been for ages," Becky informed us, following our gaze. Then she rolled her eyes and zoomed off looking cross and flustered.

Sure enough, Jan was deep in conversation with one of the customers, who had her back to us. Unusually for Jan, she was actually sitting down at the table as though she was a customer herself.

"I've never seen Jan sit down at one of the tables during the day before," commented Leah.

"Me neither," said Fen. "I wonder what's so serious that she leaves the café to Becky for all this time?"

Then the lady turned slightly and we all saw clearly who it was: Mrs Olive Stone, or Miss Wickham. My heart sank. I bet I knew exactly what she was discussing with Jan.

"Oh, no," I groaned, sliding down in my chair.

"What?" they all demanded. So I took a deep breath and began to tell my story. I started with the letter to Chris. I said exactly what was in there, and repeated several times in a very tired voice that I knew I was stupid, so I didn't need any lectures from any of them, then I explained about Mum taking back the library book with the letter still in it, and how I'd never signed it. I went on to my theory about Chris and his mates "borrowing" an exercise book from every girl in year eight to run the handwriting test, then I told them about going to the library to find out who'd taken out the book *Lisa's Dream*. I recounted how I'd stopped for an ice cream and walked into a lamppost, then poured my ice cream over a parked car, and how I'd nearly died from heart failure because the driver of the car turned out to be Mrs Olive Stone.

All the time I was talking I was aware that I held my friends beautifully spellbound, and they were all trying really hard not to make any tut-tut noises or give me any disapproving looks.

"Then I went home to find Jon there, but—"

"Stop! Hold on, Luce. That's enough for now. We can come on to Jon in a minute." That was Fen. The others were nodding in agreement. It was as though my story was too much for them to take in and they needed a break before moving on to the next thing.

"Did you find out who it was who had taken out the book with your note in it?"

"Nope."

"And what I want to know is where's Chris Harvey in all of this?" said Andy with a frown, as she stared at the table.

"That's what *I've* been asking myself," I said, feeling proud that I'd managed to be as detective-like as Andy for once.

"He might have nothing to do with it," she went on thoughtfully.

"Well, he must have got the letter," said Leah.

"Not necessarily. It depends who got the book out of the library. I mean, think about it. It's really odd that Chris hasn't once appeared, but you've seen that Luke boy three times: once when he brought those exercise books into your French lesson, once down on the netball courts yesterday morning and once in the corridor with the rest of the bully boys."

"But Chris wrote back to Luce," Jaimini said.

"Not necessarily. That might have been his friends again. Let's have a look at the letter he wrote, Luce."

"Ah. . ."

"What?" She paused and they all looked at

me. "Luce, what have you done with Chris's letter?"

"Well, I, er, I handed it in."

"You handed it in? You're mad! What d'you hand it in for? What do you think a teacher's going to think about it?"

"I thought the teacher might be mad with Chris. That was the whole idea. It's my way of getting back at him."

Andy was looking very slightly thundery – just very slightly.

"Now, hold on, Andy," said Leah, obviously reading the signs and putting a restraining hand on Andy's arm. "I get how Luce's mind is working. You see, the teacher wouldn't get cross with Luce. After all, she's only thirteen—"

"Yes, Leah's right," Fen jumped in. "But Chris would come in for a big telling off if a teacher found that note, because it's obvious he's deliberately encouraging a poor lovesick thirteen-year-old to pursue him, and they wouldn't like that one little bit."

"Excuse me, this is *me* you're all talking about here," I pointed out, sitting up straight. "And can we have less of 'Leah's right' thank you very much. It's *me* who's right, actually."

"It's *I* who's right, actually," said Jaimini, which really got to me, because she hadn't said anything at all so far.

"What a cheek!" I said, turning on her.

"Calm down, Luce, she's correcting your grammar," Andy told me, flapping her hand at me rather impatiently. Then she turned to Fen, as though I was a slightly irritating fly that she had to bat out of her way every so often so that she could get on with the infinitely more interesting job of discussing my problems with everyone but me. Great!

"That woman's going. And Jan's coming over," interrupted Leah.

Sure enough, Mrs Olive Stone was on her way out. She hadn't noticed me sitting at the table over here. Perhaps I actually *had* turned into a fly without realizing it. It certainly felt like it, the way everyone was ignoring me.

"Hello, you lot. How are you all?"

Jan smiled round the table, but I had the feeling that her mind was miles away. What was the betting that the second her gaze fell upon me, she'd suddenly come down to earth with a bump and tell me off for dropping ice cream on to customers' cars? I couldn't believe it when she got out her little notepad and said, "What can I get you all to drink today? Let's start with you, Luce." She was still smiling. Oh well, at least I knew I wasn't a fly. Unless I happened to be a fly called Luce, of course. We all gave her our orders, then off she went. Positively painless! The relief was enormous. I didn't think I could take any more aggro in one day.

"But Chris might have got absolutely nothing at all to do with any of this," Andy repeated the moment Jan had gone.

"So what?" I asked, beginning to feel exasperated, because it didn't make my problem any smaller, even if Chris was totally uninvolved.

"So, he's about to be in big trouble for something that has nothing to do with him."

"Why?"

"Because you've left a letter, apparently from him, in your French book," Andy spelt out slowly.

"Good. Serves him right," I said.

"What?"

"Well, he might have nothing to do with any of this, but the fact remains that he hangs around with those horrible mean bullies, so he can't be any better himself. I bet that's how they get their kicks, setting up nasty jokes for each other."

"Well, they hardly set this one up because you did," Jaimini pointed out.

"I know I did, but then they turned it into something horrible for Chris as well. I can just imagine how they carry on. Next time it'll be Chris playing some underhand trick on one of the others. That's how boys like that get their kicks."

"Well, you could be right," said Leah. "But what if, I mean, just supposing you're wrong?"

I was frowning and weighing up how bad this was, when Fen said, "And guess what, everybody?"

"What?"

"He's just walked in."

"Who?"

"The man in the moon. Who do you think?"

It was Chris. I felt the heat rising up my cheeks. He was scanning the place as though looking for someone. I wished the blade of a saw would suddenly come up through the carpet and start cutting a nice neat circle round our table, like you see in all the best cartoons, and then our table would go crashing down out of sight. No such thing happened. Instead, Chris's eyes met mine, and he hesitated when he realized I was surrounded by my friends, then he came over to me.

"Excuse me, are you Lucy Edmunson?"

I tried to keep in mind how horrible he was, but I could feel my heart melting at the sound of his voice. In fact, I thought my entire body was melting I felt so hot.

"Could I have a word with you for a moment, please?" he asked me. He didn't look embarrassed or anything. I felt a light tapping on my leg, and realized that Jaimini was trying to get through to me. She'd probably been whacking me for ages. As well as Jaimini's rib-digging, I'm also immune to any of her other attention-attracting tactics.

"There's a table free over there," Chris was saying, and I jumped up as though I'd been burnt, because that was the moment that I suddenly realized that Jaimini must have recognized the faraway look in my eyes, and thought she ought to try and bring me back to earth. Hence all the tapping.

If I had been told two days ago that I would now be sitting at a table in the café opposite the object of my passions, I wouldn't have believed it. Jan appeared with my Coke at that point. She put it down with a very pointed, "There you are, Lucy." She was trying to get me to look at her so she could raise her eyebrows about my new friend. I wouldn't play, though, so she asked Chris if she could get him anything and he ordered a coffee.

"Look, I'm sorry about this, but I thought I ought to warn you," he began as soon as Jan had left us. "You know that letter you wrote to me?"

I gulped and went red again. How could he sit here and talk about my wonderful love letter, which had taken me so long to compose, as though it was a part of someone's rough history notes that they didn't need any more?

"Well, the thing is, I'm afraid it seems to have fallen into the wrong hands."

"Oh." I didn't know what to say. This was all so matter-of-fact. "Did you read it, Chris?"

I loved saying his name.

"What? Oh, yes I did. I'm going out with someone else, actually. Anyway, the thing is, I think some of the guys have made up a reply and they're likely to send it to you as a joke. I thought I ought to warn you because I don't want you to get upset, or to think that it's from me. That's all."

That was *all*! That was terrible. Chris Harvey was even nicer than I'd originally thought he was, but he was going out with someone else and had no intention of writing back to me. He was dismissing me without a thought for my poor hurt feelings. What was it they called it in poems? Unrequited love. That was it. He couldn't give a five-pence piece about my unrequited love, either. And worst of all, he wasn't even looking at me as he was telling me all this. He kept glancing round the café. Presumably he was nervous in case any of his mates showed up. Suddenly I'd had enough.

"Look, it might be nothing to you, but that letter was a big thing for me. It took me ages to screw up the courage to write to you. And then my mum took the library book back, not knowing the letter was inside. And the next thing I know, my French book had disappeared, along with every other year-eight girl's French book, and then I got it back with a horrible message signed 'Chris' inside it. But the last straw happens when I'm blocked from getting to my locker by Luke and the others, giving me verbal abuse, teasing me, and generally taunting me to death. And now you're sitting here calmly, telling me you're going out with someone else. I mean, thanks a lot."

"Oh Lucy, that's terrible. I'm really sorry." He put his head in his hands for a moment. Melt, melt, melt! His head came back up. His eyes were searching my face. I had his full attention. I tipped my head to one side, going for the expression of a sixteen-year-old, and I tried to hold his gaze as long as I could. This was rapturous. It was almost worth those boys being such pains to have *this* result.

"You're not their friend, are you?" I asked, which instantly put me firmly back into the thirteen-year-old category – or eight-year-old, more like.

"Well, you know, they're OK. Sometimes they just go a bit too far, that's all. Anyway, tell me what the letter from me said."

"You don't know?"

"Of course I don't. It's their idea of a laugh

but, like I said, they've gone too far this time. What did it say?"

"Oh, just something about meeting me under the old oak tree. I didn't even know there *was* an oak tree at school."

"Just ignore the letter."

"I don't need you to tell me that, Chris," I said, giving him an I-can-handle-myself-perfectly-well-thank-you look.

"Yeah, sorry. Have you reported them?"

"No, my friend dealt with them."

"Really?" Chris looked quite surprised and more than a little bit impressed. "What's his name?"

"Andy."

"Andy what?"

"Andy Sorrell. She's the one with the short dark hair sitting over there."

"A girl! A year-eight girl dealt with those morons?" Chris was craning his neck to get a look at Andy, who was hidden from his view because Leah was leaning forwards and her hair was hanging in a curtain in front of her face. "That titchy little thing? You're kidding!"

"That's the one. Nothing scares her, you see. She's the daring one."

"Well, I'm glad you've got someone to protect you. Anyway, I'll get going now. But I just wanted to warn you that there may be more to come. The best thing is not to let it get you down. I'm going to tell Luke and the others that I've talked to you about them, and that you're going to report them the very next time anything happens." He got up. "Anyway, look after yourself."

"Oh, Chris?"

"Yeah."

"How did you know that I was Lucy Edmunson?"

"Luke told me that you'd got lots of blonde hair and freckles."

I nodded, glumly.

"He didn't mention what a nice person you are, though, or what a nice smile you've got."

My stomach did a back flip, followed by a yo-yo, and I tried not to do the obvious, but I couldn't help it. A big beam was breaking out all over my face. How naff. He could just have turned away and walked out, but he didn't. He smiled back and said, "Take care, OK?"

"OK." And then he did go.

Quite honestly, if he'd told me to swim the Channel I would have been halfway to Dover. I sat in my own little dream until Jaimini came to yank me back over to the others.

"Don't say she's fallen in love again," said Fen, closing her eyes slowly.

"What difference does it make to you?" I demanded.

"OK, OK, calm down," she replied, putting her hands up as though to surrender.

"What did he say?" asked Leah, so I told them, word for glorious word, and I think they were all quite impressed because there was a short silence at the end, before Andy spoke.

"Looks like we'd better get that letter out of your French book, doesn't it?"

"Omigod!" I said, leaping to my feet.

"There's not a lot you can do about it right now, Luce," said Jaimini, pulling me back down again.

"I bet Mr Farmer will have taken the books home with him to mark. Oh, if only I hadn't left it in there. Now poor Chris will be in trouble. I can't bear it."

"Calm down, Luce. The very worst thing that could happen would be that the Head calls him to see her and she asks him for an explanation and he tells her the truth," said Leah.

Put like that, it didn't sound too bad, but I wasn't convinced.

"What if she doesn't believe him?"

"Why don't you cross that bridge when you come to it?" suggested Leah sensibly.

I nodded and heaved a big sigh. "I think I might have some of that chocolate gâteau. Anyone want to share a piece?"

"I will," said a voice. We all looked up. There was Jon.

"Oh Jon, you came! Brilliant!"

"Hello, everybody. Hi, Jaimini. Hi, Andy."

Jaimini smiled shyly and said hello, and Andy hesitated then said hello very quietly.

"I know, it's unbelievable, isn't it?" Jon said to her, on seeing her incredulous face. "It's like the return of the prodigal son, only this son has transformed."

"What a shame," said Andy, which made Leah's eyes widen and made Fen give her a surprised look. I must admit, I was pretty shocked, too. It sounded rather rude, as though Andy preferred the old version.

"You think so?" asked Jon, and for a moment he definitely looked really pleased and quite cheeky, like the old Jon, but then he quickly pulled the sensible expression back into place.

Andy said nothing as Jon pulled up a chair from another table.

"What do you think?" I managed to whisper to her when nobody was listening.

"Certainly different," she whispered back.

"Practically reincarnated, if you ask me," I whispered back again, and I reckon Jaimini heard that because I was sure I saw her roll her eyes to the ceiling.

Chapter 7

It was great that Jon had come down to the café, but the timing was bad because I hadn't had the chance to tell my friends about what had happened earlier in the day when I'd gone home. Also, Andy had to go and babysit her little brother a few minutes later and, after she'd gone, the atmosphere felt rather uncomfortable and odd. Jon was very friendly, but the conversation never really got off the ground. It was a though he didn't fit into his new image. He'd hardly been there five minutes when he said that he'd got to go.

"I only dropped in quickly to say hello, because I had to get some stuff from Cableden stationers. I'm expecting Kirsty any time now."

"Oh good, at last I'm going to meet her," I said, a touch sarcastically.

"She's looking forward to meeting you, too."

Jon bit his lip and it was obvious he was nervous. After he'd gone, I asked the others what they thought about him.

"He's so different," said Jaimini. "I kept staring at him because I couldn't adjust to this new stepbrother of yours. He didn't seem very comfortable, did he?"

"I thought he was really nice," said Leah.

"Me, too," Fen agreed. "He did seem worried about Kirsty coming, though, didn't he?"

"Maybe she's really old or something," Leah said.

"I know, I said that," I said, thinking, *typical*.

"Yeah, and he thinks you'll think he's weird for having a girlfriend ten years old than him," Jaimini said.

"Could be more than that. Could be twenty years, you know. It does happen," said Fen.

I was beginning to get worried. If the new girlfriend was twenty years older than Jon, she'd be older than Mum, and that would be seriously weird!

"Anyway, tell us what happened when you got home today." Leah changed the subject. She must have noticed me going pale.

So I told them all about hearing his voice, and how he came rushing out when the vase hit the stairs. I mentioned how he'd checked that Mum wouldn't be back for ages, as well.

114

"What do you think?" I said at the end.

"What do you think?" asked Fen.

"I'm not sure."

"Not sure? That's not like you. How about one of your crazy theories, Luce?"

Suddenly I felt really cross. "I can't win, can I? If I come out with crazy things, you make fun of me, and if I don't come out with crazy things, you make fun of me."

"Sorry, Luce. I didn't mean to tease you, but let's face it, you do get rather dramatic at times, don't you?"

"What's he like? I missed him," said Tash, appearing at that moment and leaning over to wipe our table, so that Jan couldn't accuse her of slacking.

"He's reincarnated," replied Jaimini, giving Fen a wink, which really got to me.

"What do you mean?" asked Tash, wide-eyed.

"I'm going," I said, scraping my chair back roughly, because Jaimini was making me so angry.

"Already? What time is it?" asked Leah.

"Just gone five o'clock," Tash replied, her eyes full of worry because she can't stand it when people aren't getting on properly.

"See you tomorrow everyone."

"Can't wait to hear about Kirsty," Leah said.

"Me too," said Jaimini.

"I'll tell you all about her at break time," I said to Leah, deliberately not looking at Jaimini at all.

Outside the café I stood still and frowned. Something that someone had just said was striking a chord somewhere in my mind, but I couldn't think what it was. I went over the conversation we'd just had. Was it something about reincarnation? I thought about that for a few seconds then dismissed it. Was it about Kirsty? No, I didn't think so. Or Chris? Again, I concentrated hard for a few seconds. No, it wasn't about him. So what else had been said? Nothing.

Hang on a sec. It was coming back to me. What time was it? Just gone five o'clock. That was it. Five o'clock. And today was Thursday. A feeling of terrible guilt came over me as I plunged my hand into my pocket and pulled out a scruffy bit of paper.

Terrissed gardens. Usule place. 5 oclock. Thursday.

Oh, no! Poor little Ned. I'd completely forgotten to give Tim and Leo the letter. I'd thought about nothing but Jon and Chris and my own life since Tuesday. And now it was Thursday and it had just gone five o'clock. Ned would be waiting in the Terraced Gardens. I wondered where the usual place was. I could just picture this scruffy kid standing there looking about, excitedly wondering from which direction his new friends would be coming. I suddenly felt unbearably sorry for him and knew what I had to do.

I ran and ran, with my school bag clunking against one side of me, and a stitch in the other. If only I was fit like Andy and Fen, this would have been an effortless little jog, but as it was I could feel myself sweating, puffing and panting. It was after a quarter past when I got to the Terraces, and there was no sign of Ned, but this might not have been the "usule place". Keeping my eyes on everything around me I searched the whole park, then, just when I was emerging from a tunnel of trees and coming up over a little bridge, I thought I spotted him by one of the exits.

"Ned!" I screamed out at the top of my voice.

The boy didn't turn round.

I tried again even louder but he'd disappeared, and there was no point in running after him because he could have gone in any of three different directions and his start was just too great. I sighed a big sigh, let my school bag slide to the ground and sat down on a cut-off tree trunk, feeling for a moment like an oversized elf that had run out of energy and magic.

"I thought you said your twins were coming, not you."

My head shot up. "Ned! You're here!"

"You're late."

I got up awkwardly. "I know, and I'm really sorry."

"Huh." That noise was made with utter disgust.

"I thought I'd missed you. I thought you'd gone out of that exit. I was screaming out to someone completely different, obviously."

"That was how I knew where you were, cos of that screaming."

"I *am* sorry, Ned. I know it's no excuse but I've had quite a few things on my mind lately."

It seemed a very mature thing to say to a ten-year-old boy, but I came down to earth with his next words.

"When it got to a quarter past, I said to myself, 'Jaimini won't let me down.' But you did, didn't you?"

I was also taken aback because I'd forgotten that I'd told him I was called Jaimini.

"Look, I said I was sorry, didn't I? I've had stuff on my mind."

"Like what?"

I was about to say, "Nothing", but I suddenly thought, "Oh, what the heck?"

"Like having to put up with a lot of aggro from some year-eleven boys. Look. . ." I sat back down on the tree trunk and Ned sat on the ground. It didn't seem to worry him that it was all gravelly. "When I came across you in the library I was looking for a letter that I'd written to this boy I really like."

"Chris."

"Yeah! How did you know he was called Chris?"

He realized his mistake instantly, and came out with a sort of stammering explanation. The stammer pretty soon went, though, because Ned just wasn't the type to get ruffled or embarrassed. "I th-th-thought I'd s-s-save someone the trouble, cos I reckoned I knew who Chris was."

"I see. So, let's get this perfectly straight. You saw me in the library frantically searching for something. You let me carry on despite the fact that you knew it was a completely pointless exercise because you had already found the letter and had it in your pocket. You followed me out of the library and when I asked you whether you'd got my letter, you pretended you knew nothing about it, and you then showed me your own pathetic little letter to put me off the scent. Is that a fair summary?"

"No, cos it wasn't pathetic." He was scowling.

"Yeah, OK, sorry. But come on, Ned, you have to admit I've got a right to be cross, haven't I?"

"How come you didn't sign the letter?"

"Because I wasn't sure that I'd finished it. I just tucked it inside my library book to keep it safe and private, then my mum went and took the library book back."

"Bet you got a shock when you found it wasn't there!" He giggled.

"You're really making me mad now, Ned. You've no idea what I've had to go through because of that letter falling into the wrong hands."

"Well, that's not my fault. I thought I was doing you a favour. I gave it to Chris."

"You gave it to Chris? How do you know him?"

"Well, it's the one who goes to Cableden Comp."

"That's right, but how do *you* know him?"

"Well, he's got dark hair, he's tall, lots of girls like him and he lives near me."

"That's the one. But somewhere along the line someone else got hold of it."

"That's not my fault."

"No, I suppose not."

We both sat in silence. Ned was scraping at the gravel with the toe of his shoe. He was making overlapping circles. I was staring at them while my mind worked away. Then we both spoke at the same time.

"If I wrote another letter—"

"Should I give you another message—"

"Go on."

"You first."

"I was going to say, if I wrote another letter for Chris, could you give it to him?"

He nodded. "And same here. Your twins?"

I knew what he meant. Thousands wouldn't. So I ripped some paper out of my rough book and handed a page to Ned, along with a text book to rest on, and for a while neither of us spoke while we both worked on our masterpieces. It must have been quite a funny sight for passers-by. Not that there were any. Ned was really attacking his letter. He pressed hard, and he kind of grunted as he concentrated. It was like sitting next to a gorilla writing a letter. I couldn't concentrate on my own letter at all, and in the end I gave up. It was partly because I couldn't think, but also partly because there was really nothing left to say to Chris. I mean, let's face it, he wasn't interested in me because he'd got his own girl-friend and anyway, I was just a silly little year-eight with a nice smile as far as he was concerned.

"Finished?" I said as I watched Ned folding and folding his paper. "I don't actually think it'll go any smaller, Ned."

He had folded it into such a tight little square that it looked like a ravioli parcel.

"Don't forget this time. Where's yours?"

"I changed my mind. Just tell him I said hello when you next see him."

We both got up, and suddenly neither of us knew what to say.

"See you then."

"Bye."

And off we went in our separate directions.

All the way home I tried to decide whether to read Ned's message. In the end I did, because Ned hadn't actually told me not to. It took longer to unfold it than it did to read it.

I'm friends of your sister. She said why dont you right a letter to my twins Ned so I did. Do you want to meet me in the terissed gardens on Friday after scool or Satday morning at 11. Ill wait both times.
From Ned.
P.S. I am ten years old.

This time I must be sure to remember to give Tim and Leo the note. It was very badly written but I thought they'd be quite impressed as Ned was ten. I was glad he put that bit at the end.

Mum was in the kitchen when I got in.

"Where's Jon, Mum?"

"He's gone to the station to pick up Kirsty."

"Oh, great! Where are the boys?"

"Watching television. Where have you been?"

"I had to meet this boy in the Terraced Gardens."

"What?"

I'd shocked her. As I went back over my words, I realized why. "No, not that kind of a boy. A ten-year-old. He wanted me to give a message to Tim and Leo."

"Oh, right." She was smiling as she cut the slippery liver into small pieces.

"Hi, you two, I've got something for you," I said, as I went into the sitting room. They both glanced up, saw that I didn't appear to be carrying anything and turned back to the telly, then, about five seconds later, they looked round properly. It was always such a double act the way the twins carried on. I knew exactly how their minds had worked just then. They had thought that whatever I had got for them hadn't been worth taking any notice of because it wasn't visible, then they had realized at exactly the same moment that maybe it was money. I held out the letter and they both leapt for it. Tim got there first. He unfolded the paper quickly, with Leo watching closely, then, their heads bent forwards and touching, they scanned the message.

"Who's Ned?" they asked a few seconds later.

"This boy I met in the library. He and his friend always left messages in books for each other in the town where he used to live. He was telling me about it, and I said I thought you two might be interested in that, then I suggested he wrote to you to get it started."

"We're going to Pete Frate's after school tomorrow."

"Well, what about Saturday morning?"

"Mum'd never let us go on our own."

"I'll walk you down there."

"OK."

Just like that! Boys are funny, aren't they? If it had been me, meeting another girl, I'd be really curious to know what she looked like and every other thing about her, but Tim and Leo were already glued to the television again so I went back into the kitchen.

"I wonder what Kirsty will be like."

Mum stopped what she was doing and faced me. "We mustn't show any shock, Luce. Jon's hinted a couple of times that we might be surprised. She might be, you know, quite a bit older than Jon."

"Yeah, that's what I've been thinking. I mean, she might be as old as you, Mum."

"Exactly," said Mum, "and that's ancient!"

"No, I didn't mean that."

"I know, it's all right. But let's just make sure we don't look horrified or anything. I've already warned the twins."

We both distinctly heard a car door bang and Mum rushed to the window, glanced quickly out, then bobbed back out of sight. "It's Jon."

"What's Kirsty like?"

"Didn't see her. Sit at the table and read the newspaper. Look as though you're doing something." Mum was so nervous it was affecting me.

"Mum, if you roll that pastry any thinner it'll be in rags."

The door opened, very slowly, before she could reply. Kirsty was in front of Jon. She seemed reluctant to come in. Jon was practically pushing her from behind. I nearly gasped at the sight of her, but not because there was anything wrong or unusual about her. Quite the opposite, in fact. She was absolutely normal and really lovely, just the right age for Jon, slim and pretty with her hair like mine – kind of reddy-blonde with loads of curls. She was wearing tight black jeans and a big, loose sweater in dark orange. Her eyes were greeny-bluey-grey, just like mine, and they stared out of a pale face. She looked very worried. The moment that Kirsty walked into our kitchen is a moment that I don't think I'll ever forget. Everything seemed to stand still for a few seconds until everyone had taken stock of one another.

I wanted to look at Mum to see how she was taking the shock of there being no shock, if you get my meaning. But I didn't want to take my eyes off Kirsty and Jon. Jon had shut the door behind them and his arm was firmly around

Kirsty's shoulder. I had a weird thought at that moment. It occurred to me that there was only one possible shock left, and that was if Kirsty should turn out to be dumb.

"Hi," she said. "It's lovely to meet you both at last."

No more shocks left. So why the nervousness? Why the big build-up? Had we only imagined that something was wrong? I mean, this was perfect, wasn't it? Not for me, obviously. I wanted my scruffy actor brother back, but for Mum and Dad it couldn't be better. Their son had left behind his misspent youth, got himself a proper job and the most lovely-looking girlfriend you could imagine. Lovely? But she looked like me. She'd even got freckles! Maybe there was hope for me after all. I suddenly felt ridiculously happy.

"It's lovely to meet you, too," I said, rushing over impulsively, grabbing her hand and practically tearing her away from Jon. It turned out that that was exactly what was needed as an ice-breaker, because everybody laughed a bit nervously at my enthusiastic welcome.

"Luce!" said Mum, but she was only pretending to be shocked. "Don't drag the poor girl about so roughly when she's only just met us!"

"Yes, wait till you've known me five minutes, Luce, then you can drag me about as roughly as you like," said Kirsty, whose face had broken into a wide smile. She suddenly looked so much more relaxed. At that moment I *did* look at Mum and she gave me a wink. I understood that wink. She was saying, "Isn't Kirsty nice? Hasn't it all turned out well?"

And it was true. I couldn't believe that we'd been lucky enough to have someone who was pretty *and* witty for Jon's girlfriend – if she was his girlfriend. Oh, no! Perhaps that was the shock. Perhaps she wasn't his girlfriend at all. Maybe she was going to turn out to be his counsellor or something because he was getting over alcoholism as I had originally thought. I knew my imagination was running away with me but I couldn't help it, because I was dreading finding out that Kirsty wasn't Jon's girlfriend. I didn't think I'd ever taken to a perfect stranger quite so easily. Maybe it was because she looked like me. Whatever the reason, I desperately wanted her to be Jon's girlfriend.

I was still gripping her hand and had led her to the table to sit down. Mum had come over, too. I guess she probably felt as drawn to Kirsty as I did. Then my troubled thoughts disappeared in a flash as Terry walked in. He always has this effect on me. I'm much closer to him than I am to my real dad. Terry's more like a lovely cuddly bear than Mr Universe, and he admits that he's quite lazy, but the great thing is that you always know where you are with him. He doesn't have moods, and when he's not being lazy he attacks life with loads of opinions and ideas. I'm so pleased Mum's married to him.

It was wonderful to see him walk in at that moment. He went striding over to Kirsty, grasped her hand, and started shaking it enthusiastically.

"At long last," he said. "You must be Kirsty. I'm Terry. Hi."

"Hi," she replied with a warm smile.

Terry seemed relaxed right from the word go compared to how Mum and I had been. "Hi, darling," he said to Mum and he ruffled my hair as though I was about three, but I didn't mind. "Glass of wine everybody? I could certainly do with one after the day I've had."

"Oh dear, was it bad?" Mum asked.

"No, I just want an excuse for a glass of wine," Terry laughed. This was typical Terry wit. "Let's have some crisps, too. I need building up," he added, patting his stomach, which has been rather tubby ever since I've known him, but was definitely getting even tubbier these days.

Kirsty was laughing. "I'd love a glass of wine," she said.

"Red, white or blue?" said Terry, which was what he always said. It was just his little joke.

"White, thank you."

Good old Terry. He was making everything so relaxed. A moment later he was proposing a toast. "To the arrival of Kirsty!" Then he took a big gulp and smacked his lips appreciatively. "Where are those two reprobates?"

"Watching TV."

"Come and say hello to your old dad and your new friend," yelled Terry, in the general direction of the door.

A moment later Tim and Leo came crashing into the kitchen and wound their thin arms round Terry's neck, Tim trying to force his way on to Terry's lap at the same time. Neither of them seemed remotely interested in Kirsty. They threw her a quick glance then concentrated on Terry.

"You're far too big for all that," Terry joked.

"No, it's you who's far too big!" Tim replied, which raised another laugh.

And then it happened. The shock I had been waiting for suddenly arrived, and burst in on my happy, relaxed mind like a roaring lion in a peaceful glade. Kirsty's left hand was resting on the table, and on the fourth finger was a plain gold band. Kirsty was married!

Chapter 8

Breakfast on Friday morning was much the same as any other breakfast. The twins never talk much in the mornings. They're always more than a bit grumpy, in fact, and this morning was no exception. Mum was buttering toast. I was on the lookout for any signs of tension, but there were none. I didn't think that she (or anyone else, come to that), had noticed the ring on Kirsty's finger. Mum and Dad both looked perfectly relaxed. I was dreading them finding out that Kirsty was married.

If only I hadn't seen that ring I would have really enjoyed the previous evening. It turned out that Kirsty had been at the same drama college as Jon. That's where they'd met. She'd been working in a theatre bookshop since then and she'd also managed to get a sort of medium-sized role in a television film, so she must have been pretty talented. Apparently she was more of a serious actress while Jon had mainly done comedy. I didn't know how Jon could bear to think of all he was missing now that he had given up acting to be in a boring job.

While Jon had been having one conversation with Mum and Terry, I'd been quizzing Kirsty about the television film and loads of other things. She told me she'd recently given up work to look after her mother, and I was about to ask why when Jon drew her into his conversation with Mum and Terry, so I never did find out.

On that Friday morning Jon and Kirsty hadn't come down for breakfast, so I guessed I wouldn't see them before school.

"So, what are you up to today, Lucy?" Terry asked me brightly.

"School, café, home," I summarized quickly. "She's nice, isn't she? Kirsty, I mean," I said.

"Absolutely lovely," Mum agreed, as she munched her toast and tried to read the back of Terry's paper.

"What do you think?" Terry asked me, slapping his paper down unexpectedly.

"Yeah, lovely, I agree. Only I can't work out why Jon seemed so worried about bringing her here," I said carefully.

"Jon's very lucky to have a nice-looking

girlfriend that's got good clothes and every-thing," Tim informed everyone.

"I quite agree," said Terry. "I wouldn't mind a nice-looking girlfriend like that myself, actually!"

"Nobody but Mum would put up with your big belly," Leo told him in a matter-of-fact voice.

"That's probably true," Terry agreed. "One day I'll go on a diet. Promise."

The twins groaned, and so did Mum and I. Terry was always saying he was going on a diet, but he never did.

"I must be off," he suddenly said, jumping up. He went out to get his briefcase and Mum followed him.

"What's that on your shirt?" asked Leo, when all our goodbyes had finished.

I looked down to see a huge blob of marmalade. When I flicked it off it left a stain that I stupidly rubbed with my hand.

"You can't wear that shirt. Get another one and put that one in the wash," Mum instructed me briskly. But there wasn't another one ironed and by the time I'd found one and got the ironing board out and ironed it, I realized I was going to be late for school.

When I'd run non-stop for about five minutes I decided that if I was going to be late I might as well be really late because, as usual, I'd got a stitch, so I slowed right down and strolled along, not caring. It was five past nine when I walked along the deserted corridor towards my form room. I didn't know why I was bothering to go there really because everyone was obviously still in assembly and then it would be straight to the first lesson, which for me was biology. When I got to the form room I was about to go straight past it and on to the science lab when I caught sight of someone sitting in the room. Pushing the door open slowly I realized that whoever it was was crying. Then I got the shock of my life, because I saw that it was Jaimini.

"Jaimes, whatever's the matter?"

"Don't ask questions that you know the answer to, and don't call me that name again. You're not my friend now, you know!" I couldn't believe what I was hearing. I really didn't know what she was on about. "I don't know how you could be so horrible," she went on. "If this is paying me back just because of what I said about reincarnation, you must need your head examined. You must have known what could have happened, after what happened to you."

"Jaimini, I really don't know what you're talking about, I promise."

"Yes, you do," she replied, wiping her hand aggressively across her eyes and giving me a hard stare.

At that moment I heard a voice in the corridor

and turned quickly to see if they were all coming out of assembly. They weren't. It was just a couple of boys crossing into another corridor at the end of the one I was standing in. One of them must have caught sight of me out of the corner of his eye, because he turned to see who it was, then he immediately whispered to his friend and they both disappeared from view. They must have been more of Chris Harvey's "sort-of" friends. The next minute I was practically flattened against the door by Jaimini rushing out, not caring that she'd banged into me.

"Jaimes—"

"I said don't call me that!"

I just stared after her disappearing back and wondered what on earth was going on and what had happened to make her act like this towards me. Maybe the others would be able to tell me when they came out of assembly. The trouble was, I wouldn't see anyone till second period, which was French. Oh well, not long to wait, I thought, as I went shuffling along to biology, head down, deep in thought.

"What's up with Jaimini?" were my first words to Leah as she walked into French just ahead of Fen and Tash. For once I'd arrived first.

She looked at me blankly and I didn't have time to ask the other two because Mr Farmer was there, handing back our French exercise books. I felt my stomach turn over as I remembered what I'd left in mine. I watched Mr Farmer to see if there was any sign of him being angry. He appeared to be acting completely normally. He'd dumped the exercise books on the three front people's desks and asked them to pass them back. The moment I got mine I turned straight to the front and saw that the letter was still there. I glanced up at Mr Farmer. Our eyes met. I was expecting him to look cross or at least frown, but I was totally thrown because he smiled at me as though he found the whole thing very amusing.

"Yes, some of your books made very interesting reading," he said to the class in general, but I knew he was referring to mine in particular. I couldn't believe it. Mr Farmer thought the whole thing was a big joke. We carried on with the French lesson, and when it came to vocab about gardens and flowers, he very pointedly asked me what the French for "oak tree" was. I could have died of embarrassment. I said I didn't know and he told me the answer with a big grin on his face. When he saw that I wasn't grinning back I think he decided to call it a day because, for the rest of the lesson, he didn't give me any more looks of amusement and he didn't make any more references to oak trees or anything I could have connected with the fateful letter.

At morning break I couldn't find the others on

the netball courts so I came back up to the school. I looked everywhere, and then went back down to the netball courts and found them all there, except Jaimini.

"Where've you been? I've been looking for you everywhere," I began. "Where's Jaimini?"

"She's with Mrs Merle."

"Mrs Merle? Why?" At this point I realized that the atmosphere was rather frosty. I looked at Tash because she could usually be relied upon to be nice and normal, no matter how anyone else was acting. Not this time. Tash was sitting with her head down, her hair hanging over her face. I looked at Andy, but I didn't like the look she gave me back, and Fen was wearing the same expression. Leah was the only one who managed to give me something resembling a welcome. I raised my eyebrows at her and she got up. Without a word she began to walk away from the others and I walked with her.

"What's going on?" I asked her as soon as we were out of earshot. "Why is everyone acting like I've just tortured their favourite pets?"

"Because of Jaimini."

"What do you mean? What's happened to Jaimini? Can't you just tell me what's going on?"

"Jaimini had to put up with those nasty year-eleven boys this morning and she's not as easy-going as you are. Things like that upset Jaimini.

They got her on her own going into school and stood round her, teasing her about Chris Harvey."

"What? Chris Harvey? But—"

"Why ever did you want to get Jaimini involved, Luce? She's your best friend. I know she was a bit sarcastic about Jon, but I can't believe you paid her back like you did."

"I swear I don't know what you're on about, Leah. Why were those boys taking the mickey out of Jaimini? They know it's me who fancies Chris Harvey."

"But you told them it was Jaimini."

"No I didn't, honestly."

"OK, you didn't tell them directly, but you gave some kid a message to say 'Hello from Jaimini' to Chris Harvey."

"Omigod!"

"So it's true?" She was staring at me with her shoulders hunched and her eyebrows all knitted.

"Yeah," I said with a huge sigh.

"Oh, Luce. How could you? I thought you'd tell me it was all a lie or a mistake or a misunderstanding or something. I've been sticking up for you in front of the others. I said that you'd asked me what was the matter with Jaimini in French, and that you'd seemed genuinely not to know, and I believed you. The others are all really angry on Jaimini's behalf, but I decided to give you the benefit of the doubt. Even Tash thought I was crazy."

"But it *was* a misunderstanding."

"Save your breath, Luce." Leah was running off in the direction of the netball courts. She had sounded so sad and so angry at the same time. That was nothing to how I felt. What an utter mess! All because I'd forgotten to tell Ned what my real name was. This was going to be totally impossible to explain to anyone. And who would believe me? It would all sound so far-fetched. As for that kid, Ned, I could happily have killed him. He must have been about as discreet as Big Ben. I could just imagine him making some big announcement to Chris, in front of all his friends. I must remember never *ever* to be taken in by boys under the age of fourteen again.

History began to repeat itself as the bell went and I slipped out of the gap in the hedge again. There seemed no point at all in staying at school. Maybe the ice-cream van would be there again and I could buy an ice cream, only this time I'd try not to drop it over any parked vehicles. A run-in with Mrs Olive Stone would be all I needed. All the same, the library was a good idea. There might even be a reply to my letter waiting for me. I quickened my pace, because it was good to have something to look forward to in the middle of this awful time I was having.

As I went towards the teenage section I got a funny look from one of the librarians, and realized that she was probably getting slightly suspicious about seeing me out of school twice in my school uniform. I gave her a nice smile and hoped that she would feel a bit less suspicious as I seemed so relaxed, then I rounded the corner and set about hauling out all the books by authors beginning with D. On the fourth book I struck lucky. Inside the front cover was a piece of paper with "SF" written on it. Yes! I unfolded it and read the following message.

Dear SF,

I was really happy and excited to receive your message. I've been trying to imagine what you're like. I am thirteen, too. I quite like school, but my best friend doesn't particularly, and *we* get on fine most of the time, so I expect you and I will too. Please write back and tell me a bit more about yourself. Put your reply in a book by an author beginning with W.

From LF.

My eyes were shining by the time I got to the end. This girl sounded so nice. I felt a tiny stab of jealousy that she'd got a best friend. I hoped it wouldn't be too long before I got Jaimini back as my best friend, but I didn't really know if things would ever be the same between us again, because I'd never be able to convince her that I hadn't deliberately dropped her in it. I clutched my letter as I left the library and wondered what to do next. I'd only got two choices, home or school, and just like the last time, I chose home. I planned to get back to school by lunch time again. Maybe I'd tell Mum all that had happened and see what she suggested I should do.

This thought cheered me up slightly and I felt even better when I saw that her car was there. Jon's was there, too. As I passed it, I glanced in and noticed a photo on the passenger seat. I couldn't resist trying the car door to see if it was locked. Surprisingly it wasn't, so I opened it and took out the photo.

It was of Kirsty and a man. It looked as though they were standing in front of a register office. I stared at the photo in utter disbelief. Kirsty was carrying flowers and was dressed in a cream suit. The man wore a dark-coloured suit and he was hugging her close to him. He looked to be a couple of years older than Kirsty and they were both smiling happily. So I'd been right all along. Kirsty *was* married. How could she deceive this poor man by going out with Jon? And how could Jon be so horrible? The photo looked to be fairly recent. They must only have been married for a short time. And what on earth was it doing in Jon's car? It suddenly felt as though the photo was burning my hand. I chucked it back on to the passenger seat, shut the car door and went inside to find Mum washing up pans. She was running the hot tap hard and didn't hear me at first. She nearly jumped out of her skin when I said her name.

"Whatever are you doing here, Luce?"

"It's a long story."

She stopped what she was doing, turned off the tap, dried her hands and put them on my shoulders. "Come on, then. Let's hear it." Her expression was a mixture of kindness and strictness, and I told her about the whole Jaimini, Chris and Ned thing. She was very sympathetic but didn't have any bright ideas about what I should do. I could tell she thought I oughtn't to have come home from school without telling anyone, and she was quick to say that I really should get back there and face the music.

By now I felt really depressed. My stepbrother was going out with a married woman, all my friends hated me, the only boy I fancied was going out with someone else and all his friends were having a field day taking the mickey out of me.

I was about to set off back to school when Jon and Kirsty came into the kitchen. They both looked tense, but they were trying not to. They also looked as though they might just have had an argument with each other. I glanced at Mum, but she seemed just as delighted with everything as she had done the day before. It was all roses as far as she was concerned. I couldn't help my eyes straying to Kirsty's left hand, and you can imagine the shock I got when I saw that the ring was missing. As I looked up again, my eyes met Kirsty's, and she gave me a searching look. I know I blushed but I couldn't help it.

For the next few seconds I couldn't concentrate, but when I tuned back into the conversation it was to hear Mum asking Kirsty about her parents.

"My mother died – very recently, actually," Kirsty said. She looked at Jon as though asking for his help and I suddenly felt very sorry for her. Mum did, too, I could tell. So this was why Kirsty had told me she'd been looking after her mother.

"I'm so sorry, Kirsty. Had she been ill?"

"She died of multiple sclerosis. She'd had it for years."

"I'm so sorry," Mum repeated, and she was on the point of saying something else when Kirsty said, "Jon met her, didn't you, Jon?"

"Y-Yes, I did," stammered Jon. "She was a remarkable woman. I don't know how anyone can begin to live with such a terrible illness."

"It must take enormous courage," Mum agreed.

"We held an evening at the drama college, actually," said Jon. "You know, all sorts of different acts, and all the money went to multiple sclerosis research."

"Oh, so you're still in touch with the college then?" Mum asked.

"Yes, we are," Jon answered, and I saw a frown cross Mum's face, but it soon went when Jon and Kirsty started telling us about some of the comic acts. I found it hysterically funny. Jon hadn't lost any of his old drama ability. It made me mad to think of the waste of his talent now he was in some boring management job.

Unfortunately Mum insisted that I should get back to school after about ten minutes of this. Jon offered to take me but I wanted to be alone with my thoughts.

Kirsty knew that *I* knew that she was married. It was perfectly obvious that this was the reason for all the tension between her and Jon. It was also perfectly obvious that Mum hadn't noticed, so now I was the only one who knew their secret. The more I thought about the situation the more I felt cross. Why couldn't they be honest with us? I'd liked Kirsty so much at first, and now I felt all my old bad feelings from before I'd even met her coming back. She'd taken Jon and changed him. She'd somehow cast a spell over him so he'd stay devoted to her, even though she was married to someone else. If it hadn't been for Kirsty, I felt sure that Jon wouldn't have left college and joined the world of boring adults. He was so wishy-washy now, except for that brief glimpse of the old Jon that I'd seen when he'd been imitating the comic acts from the multiple sclerosis evening.

I wished things could go back to how they'd been before all of this happened. It was hard to be friendly towards Jon and Kirsty when I knew they were keeping a big secret from us all. The only good thing in my life at this moment was my library friend.

Chapter 9

Once again, I slipped back into school without anyone noticing my absence, as far as I knew. I was on the point of rushing off to find the others when I remembered that they weren't friends with me, so I went into the IT room and sat down at one of the computers. There, I took out a piece of paper and wrote to my new library friend.

Dear LF,

Thank you for your letter, which I got this morning. I know I should have been in school really, but I kind of ran away because none of my friends like me at the moment. In a way it's my own fault, because I got my best friend into trouble with a gang of horrible year-eleven boys. The thing is, I didn't mean to, obviously. I won't tell you the whole story but I'll just tell you how the problem arose in the first place. You see, I met this boy called Ned in the library, and at the time it was important that he didn't know my name, so I just said the first name that came into my head, which was my best friend's name. Anyway, because I did that, I've got my best friend into trouble, and I don't know how to make her believe that it was just a mistake.

Something else bad is happening in my family too, and maybe one day I'll tell you about that, but for now I can only really tell my best friend, so I'll just have to tell nobody until we're friends again. It feels really weird saying all this to someone I've never even met!

Can't wait to get your next letter.

from,

SF.

PS: put your reply in a book by any author beginning with M.

I saw Jaimini and the others during the afternoon but I didn't really speak to them. It made me sad, in a way. Tash and Leah both made a bit of an effort to talk to me, but the others didn't. I decided that I'd get the weekend over with and then I'd try and talk to Jaimini on Monday – maybe she would have calmed down a bit by then. I think I would have been much more upset about not being friends if I didn't have my head filled with thoughts about Jon and Kirsty.

As soon as school was finished I went straight to the library. The others all went one way and I went off another. Tash was unhappy about it, I could tell, but there didn't seem to be anything I could do about that. When I saw that kid, Ned, I would brain him for not thinking before opening his big mouth in front of all Chris's friends. If only he'd been sensible and chosen a nice quiet moment when Chris was all on his own, I wouldn't be in so much trouble now. The trouble was that, much as I wanted to pin the blame for everything on to Ned, I knew in my heart that I couldn't, because he's only ten after all, and I shouldn't have trusted him with something as personal as a message to an older boy. Also, I couldn't blame Ned for saying that the message was from Jaimini, because that was my fault for not thinking before I opened my big mouth. I couldn't help smiling as I thought this, because if you think about it, Ned and I had quite a lot in common. Neither of us had thought before opening our big mouths!

I put my message into a book by an author

called Diane Wynstone, and got another funny look from the librarian. I suppose she was wondering why I kept going in and out without exchanging any books.

When I got home, Mum was in the garden, digging. She loves gardening, but she wasn't loving it this afternoon – she was digging away ferociously and I knew something was wrong, but I didn't know what. It crossed my mind that maybe Jon and Kirsty had confessed their secret. I offered to help her, so for the next half-hour we both got rid of our tensions.

"It's nice having Kirsty here, isn't it?" I began tentatively, to see if this was the problem.

"Yes, she really is a gem." Mum was smiling was she was digging and I could tell immediately that she didn't know that Kirsty was married. In that case, Mum's problem must be nothing to do with that, and I decided not to pry any further, so for a while we didn't talk at all. Then Mum said, "I expect you're quite disappointed that you can't talk about acting with Jon any more?"

She wasn't looking at me and was trying to sound casual, but I knew Mum, and she was leading up to something. Maybe she sensed that I preferred the old Jon.

"I do miss the old Jon," I said carefully, after a few seconds.

There was another long pause, then Mum surprised me by saying. "Yes, me too ... and Terry."

I gasped and fell back on to my bottom, which made Mum laugh, but not me. I was too shocked.

"You mean, you're not over-the-moon delighted by this job of Jon's? I can't believe it. You and Terry were always getting at him about doing drama and what a waste of time it was."

"We weren't always getting at him! He was never here to be got at, but it was true that we weren't particularly happy about the kind of life he was leading."

"So why aren't you happy now then?" I asked.

"It's not that we aren't happy. It's just that we suddenly find we miss the old Jon, just like you do. The old Jon might have been scruffy and lazy, but he had guts and tons of character. The new Jon is perfectly nice and respectable, but there seems to be something missing and I can't quite put my finger on what it is. Kirsty is so lovely and yet Jon seems, well, sad, I suppose."

At that moment I decided to mention the photo I'd seen in Jon's car because I suddenly *had* to tell someone.

"I saw this photo of Kirsty. It was on the passenger seat of Jon's car and I couldn't resist taking a closer look," I told Mum a little shamefacedly. She stopped digging. "It was actually of Kirsty and a man. They were standing in front of a register office, smiling and hugging each other. Kirsty was dressed in a cream suit and carrying a bouquet of flowers and the man was wearing a dark suit. What's happening, Mum? I can't bear to think about it."

Mum's face looked pale but she was pretending not to be shocked. "I'm sure there must be some explanation, although, well, they *do* seem to be very tense all the time. Maybe Terry and I should talk to them. I'll have a word with Terry tonight and we'll find a good time to broach the subject with Jon and Kirsty, but don't you say anything to either of them, will you, Luce?"

I shook my head, and thought how much I would have liked to be a fly on the wall during this talk between Mum and Terry and Jon and Kirsty.

The following morning Mum was going into town, and she said she'd drop the twins off at the Terraced Gardens at eleven o'clock, then pick them up about an hour later. I was pleased that Tim and Leo had remembered about Ned, because there was no way *I* would have remembered, with everything else that was going on in my head.

Meanwhile, I walked down to the café because, in a funny sort of way, I wanted to bump into Jaimini and try and sort things out. Jan was in her sergeant-majorish mode again and I thought

150

that this might not, after all, be such a good moment for me to be here.

As I sat there on my own I started to daydream about what a great idea it would be to have an event in the café to raise money for multiple sclerosis. I kept on thinking about all the funny stuff that Jon had showed us in our kitchen, and imagined him doing that right here, in the café. It would go down brilliantly. Jon and Kirsty could be the star turns. Jon could do his comic act and Kirsty could do something more serious. The more I thought about this plan, the better it seemed. I'd be friends with the others by then, and Leah could play her violin. This was definitely getting more and more exciting – a real brainwave. I decided to approach Jan about it, even though she seemed to be so wound up. Maybe my idea would put her in a better mood. I certainly didn't have the patience to wait until Monday before asking her. I wanted to know right there and then. So I did.

"When you've worked out some details, let me know," she said briskly, after I'd told her what I wanted. "I'm a bit busy at the moment. Sorry." Then she whizzed off into the kitchen and I was left standing there. I sat down at one of the tables, because I felt suddenly as though I'd come to a dead end. How could I work out any details? How could I do anything without my friends? I needed Jaimini's help. I was useless on my own.

The only thing I could think of was to have a sort of entertainment evening with people doing turns. For example, Leah could play her violin. Maybe there could be a raffle and a bran tub, and maybe all the money that people spent on food and drink could go to the cause as well. That would mean that Jan would really have to believe in it or she wouldn't dream of putting a lot of work and hard-earned profits into it.

It suddenly struck me that I'd never even mentioned to Jan what the worthy cause was. I'd just said that my brother had done a fantastic evening in aid of charity at his old drama college and I'd thought it would be great to do something similar in the café. I'd never mentioned the words multiple sclerosis; I was so thick at times. I'd have to go back to Jan now, and tell her which charity I was talking about.

I looked round and caught sight of her whirling round like a tornado at a million miles per hour. No, this would not be a good time to try and attract her attention. I'd just have to come back later and risk seeing all the others there. We often come in on a Saturday afternoon, you see. What a waste of time this morning was turning out to be! I was on the point of getting up and dragging myself back home when who should walk in to the café but Jaimini.

"Terry said he thought you'd be here," she said, sitting down beside me.

I couldn't believe she was talking to me normally, as though nothing had happened. I just stared and waited.

"I thought I ought to find you so that you could tell me the bad thing that is happening in your family."

"What?" I recognize these words from somewhere but I couldn't think where. Then I remembered – my letter. I'd written it in my letter to my library friend. However did Jaimini get hold of that?

"But how—"

"I've just come from the library."

"And don't tell me," I said, with mounting depression and embarrassment, "you just happened to pick up a book by Diane Wynstone."

"No, I didn't just happen to pick it up. I was looking for a message but I didn't know which book by an author beginning with W it would be in."

She was smiling, and my amazingly slow-to-catch-on brain was finally making the connection. "You mean you're—"

"LF, yes – whatever that stands for."

"It stands for Luce's Friend."

"Well, it's not right then, is it?" said Jaimini.

"Are you still angry?" I asked. "I swear it was a mistake."

"No, I'm not angry. You don't have to explain. You explained in the message, remember. As soon as I read it, I felt really terrible and I went straight to a phone box and phoned you, only Terry answered and said you were down here, so I ran all the way."

"What a relief! I couldn't bear it when I was all on my own, and then everything was going wrong at home. What did you mean when you said that LF wasn't right?"

"It should be LBF – Luce's Best Friend."

"Yeah, and JBF instead of SF," I said, feeling happy again.

"What is SF by the way?"

"Stranger's Friend."

"You're crazy!"

"What's new?"

We both laughed and laughed at the coincidence of it all. Then we got serious and I told Jaimini the whole saga of Jon and Kirsty, Kirsty's mother, and finally the photo of Kirsty with the other man. Jaimini listened wide-eyed and didn't make any comment at all, except to apologize for making fun of me before. She said she realized that she'd been really horrible and that she didn't know how I'd put up with her. It was so lovely to have my best friend back and we started making plans for our special evening at the café. About halfway through our discussions, in walked

Leah and Andy. They both looked taken aback at the sight of Jaimini and me sitting together, so we beckoned to them to come over. It didn't take Jaimini a minute to explain to the others what had happened with Ned.

"The only thing I don't understand is why you used my name in the first place?" she asked at the end.

"Because I'd pretended to this kid that the letter wasn't from me, and I was pretty convinced that he'd taken it, so when he asked me what my name was, I just said the first thing that came into my head, which was Jaimini. You see, at that time I'd forgotten that I hadn't actually signed the letter anyway. Then later, when I didn't think it would make any difference whether Ned knew I liked Chris or not, I stupidly told him that it had been me who had written the letter. Of course, I'd completely forgotten by then that I'd said my name was Jaimini."

"Oh well, who cares, as long as you're friends again," said Leah.

"What about Jon?" asked Andy.

So for the second time that day I found myself talking about the photo in Jon's car and about the ring on Kirsty's finger, as well as about the tension between Jon and Kirsty. Then Fen and Tash appeared, so once again the Café Club were all together, and between us, Jaimini and I

155

told the other four all about Jon and Kirsty. Everybody agreed that the fundraising evening was a brilliant idea, and Fen thought that maybe we ought to try and approach Jan again when I said that Jan hadn't been all that bothered the first time I'd mentioned the idea.

"Look, she's not all that busy at the moment. Do you want me to say something, Luce?"

"Yes, all right."

We watched and tried to lip-read as Fen talked to Jan across the café, and Jan answered. She didn't look too happy, and Fen came back saying that Jan wasn't all that keen because she'd already promised someone a charity evening for a very good cause, and she didn't feel that she could stretch to two.

"Did you tell her what the cause was?" Jaimini asked Fen.

"No, I don't think I did mention that," said Fen, looking a bit embarrassed, so I quickly told her that I'd made exactly the same mistake. At that precise moment Jan happened to be whizzing past the back of Fen's chair, so Fen impulsively leaned back and grabbed Jan's apron. The rest of us all cringed because Fen really wasn't thinking straight. Jan was not going to be impressed.

"It's for multiple sclerosis, Jan," was all Fen said. Just like that! We all braced ourselves for a big lecture, but to everyone's surprise Jan broke into a smile and said, "Oh well, that's exactly what the other lady wanted me to support. I was talking to her the other day, and she was explaining that her sister died of MS about a year ago. Why don't you get together with her, Luce? I'm sure she'd been keen to join forces."

"But I don't even know her," I said.

"Yes, you do. You flicked your olive stone at her, remember?"

Oh, no! Big groan. Not Mrs Olive Stone.

"I think perhaps we'll manage on our own," I said to the others when Jan had gone.

"But you can't, Luce, because Jan's made it quite clear that she's not going to have two fund-raising evenings, so you've got to talk to your Olive Stone Lady, I'm afraid," Jaimini told me gently.

"And here she is," said Andy. "Go on, Luce. strike while the iron is hot."

Oh, great. I waited till she'd sat down and got a cup of tea in front of her, then Jaimini and I went over and joined her.

"You're not going to aim any missiles at me or cover me with ice cream, are you?" she asked me, with not even the glimmer of a smile. I'd heard of dry humour, but this was positively shrivelled up.

"We wanted to talk to you about MS," I said, getting straight to the point.

"Oh?" she said, and I had her full attention. So I told her about my brother's girlfriend's mother and she was very sympathetic and immediately said that she'd love to help us. I could tell that I went up about ten points in her estimation, so I wasn't too worried when I tripped over her handbag as we were going back to our own table. It would have been OK if that had been all that had happened, but unfortunately the handbag fell open and the entire contents spilled all over the place, and my other foot – the one that hadn't kicked the handbag – kicked her powder compact and sent it flying across the floor like a rocket, straight into a table leg. The powder compact cracked open, and pinky brown powder dusted an unsuspecting man's shoes. He looked down and an expression of disgust came over his face. He then looked round to see who the clumsy idiot was who had caused this sad state of affairs.

I was on the point of going over to apologize when Mrs Olive Stone told me to go and sit down, saying that she would handle it. I didn't sit down straight away. Jaimini and I picked up the contents of her handbag and put them back, then sat down. We could hear what Mrs Olive Stone was saying to the man whose shoes were covered with her face powder.

"I'm so sorry. My young friend has two left

feet, but she also has a very big heart, so I hope you'll forgive her. I'll get a damp cloth from the kitchen for your shoes."

"Oh, right, yes, no problem," said the man. Why couldn't *I* think of clever things about feet and hearts to say to cross men?

I got home at lunch time to find Mum, Terry, Jon and Kirsty sitting round our kitchen table. The moment I walked in I knew I was interrupting something. The atmosphere was uncomfortable. I said "Hi" and started to walk through to the sitting room, but Kirsty said, "No, I think Luce should hear this, too."

"Hear what?" I asked, sitting down. All I could actually hear was my heart thumping because I had a good idea what Kirsty and Jon were about to tell us – that Kirsty was already married. I couldn't help glancing at the fourth finger on her left hand and, sure enough, the ring had reappeared.

"This isn't going to be easy," Jon said, "because I've handled the whole thing badly from the word go. Kirsty's been trying to get me to tell you the truth for the past six weeks."

"Six weeks!" I couldn't help squeaking.

"My mother adored Jon," said Kirsty softly. "One day I overheard her say to my father that she would die happy if she knew that Jon and I would be getting married. We'd already talked about getting married but we'd not planned on doing it for ages. When I told Jon what I'd heard Mum say, he said, 'Why don't we get married straight away?' We knew Mum had very little time left and Jon was certain that you two would be totally against him marrying so quickly."

"I thought you'd assumed it was just another stupid impulsive drama thing, you see," explained Jon.

"Jon said that if we invited you to our wedding you would be put in an awkward position because you wouldn't be able to say no, despite the row and everything. So he thought it would be better not to invite you at all. Here comes the difficult bit."

"We got married a month ago with just Kirsty's parents and her brother as witnesses," Jon took over. "The wedding was at a register office, and Kirsty's mother died two days after."

I gasped. Kirsty *was* married, but she was married to my brother! As usual, I'd jumped to completely the wrong conclusion when I'd noticed the ring on her wedding finger. Kirsty was biting her lip and there were tears in her eyes. Jon held her hand and carried on the incredible story.

"We planned to have a wedding in church with both our families and all our friends, but Kirsty has been on and on at me to come here and confess everything to you. She refused to come here and meet you until I'd done it, but I kept chickening out, so in the end she came along to force me into it. Neither of us could bear the lie we were living and for me, the lie was even worse, because my job . . . well, it's just not me. You see, I thought you'd approve of me more if I had a 'proper' job. I thought you'd think that I was doing something with my life, but the truth is, I hate it. It's boring. In fact, I don't know how I'm going to manage to carry on with it."

"Oh Jon, you've completely misunderstood us," Mum said, looking really upset. "We were only worried that you weren't committed enough to your drama and that you were just using the drama college as an excuse to doss about."

"So you wouldn't mind if I went back to drama?"

"No, of course not, but isn't it too late?"

"I won't let it be too late! If I set my mind on something, believe me, I go all out to get it!"

I couldn't believe what I was hearing. All the fight and the spark were back. And drama was coming back, too! I couldn't have been happier.

"You see, I stupidly thought that you might take our news better if you saw that I'd changed, that I was more responsible. . ."

Jon trailed off and I glanced nervously at Terry. He was just sitting there, still as a statue, as though in shock.

"What do you think about Jon going back to college, Kirsty?" he eventually asked, very softly.

"I never wanted him to give it up in the first place. I couldn't understand why on earth he was playing out this whole ridiculous charade. I mean, look at him. He's not right like this, is he? I thought he must have monsters for parents when he told me how he was going to try and please them by giving up college and getting a good job. When I met you both I thought Jon was even crazier, because you were both so reasonable and lovely, and I've been trying to tell him ever since to be true to himself *and* to you. But he insisted that you wouldn't understand, and when he chickened out of telling you that we were married as well, I wanted to throttle him. It's caused a fair few arguments between us, I can tell you."

We were all looking at Terry, as though waiting for his judgment. As Kirsty had been speaking his face had started to form into a very gentle smile, but still he didn't say anything.

"What do you think, Dad?" Jon finally had to ask him.

"I think you've got yourself a very wise and lovely wife," said Terry. "And I also think, thank goodness you're packing up that boring-sounding job and getting back to what we've always known you're best at."

Jon shut his eyes for a second as though he

was relieved that the verdict was "not guilty". Mum and Terry looked at each other and smiled.

Then Mum spoke to Terry. "We were right then."

"We certainly were."

Jon and Kirsty looked as puzzled as I felt.

"You mean you guessed all along that we were married?"

"Well, we had a good idea, yes, but then Lucy threw us off the scent by coming across a photo in your car."

Again Jon and Kirsty frowned as though trying to recall what photo that could possibly be, then Kirsty burst out laughing. "Oh, no!" she spluttered. "You saw the photo of me and my brother and you put two and two together and made five."

"I thought you were married to someone else," I admitted sheepishly.

"Oh, Luce, I can't bear to think of how hurt you must have felt," said Kirsty, and she jumped up and gave me a big hug. Then everyone was hugging everyone else and Terry was cracking open a bottle of champagne.

"I can't believe this. You really are the most unbelievable parents," Jon said, shaking his head in happy amazement.

"Now you know we don't normally keep a bottle of champagne in the fridge, don't you?"

Terry said as he handed round the glasses. "And that's the proof that we suspected your news, isn't it?"

"Incredible," said Jon, still shaking his head in disbelief.

"Here's to the happy couple," said Terry, raising his glass.

"And here's to having my brother back," I said. "I couldn't stand that manager guy, you know," I added, which made everybody laugh.

"I'll drink to that," said Terry. "And if you want to know, Helen and I couldn't stand that 'manager guy', as Luce puts it, either!"

"I told you, didn't I?" said Kirsty, wagging a finger at Jon.

"OK, I admit it, I totally messed up," said Jon, then he rushed out of the kitchen. Less than a minute later he was back wearing the holiest pair of faded jeans you ever saw, with a sloppy brown sweater that was all pulled out of shape. He'd messed up his hair and had nothing on his feet.

"That better?" he asked, and we all cheered and clapped. Then he turned to me and, out of the blue, he asked me this question:

"Do you remember that Christmas when I taught you that song about the frog and the mouse, Luce?"

"'Frog went a-courtin'? Course I remember. How did it go?"

Between the two of us we remembered all the words and then we had an absolutely hysterical time singing it, together with all the ridiculous actions. I played the part of the frog who was trying to get Miss Mouse to marry him. Jon was Miss Mouse. Jon's so talented. I don't know how he did it, but he somehow gave the impression that he really was a shy little mouse. By the time we'd sung the whole song, everyone was laughing hysterically, and the twins, who had come in by then, were collapsing over each other in fits of uncontrollable giggles.

"Talk about laughing like a drain," said Terry, through his snorts of laughter.

"I've often wondered how a drain laughs," I said.

"Like this," Jon informed me, and then he contorted his face and came out with the strangest gurgly sound you ever heard, which made everyone laugh again, but not half as much as they had done for the frog song. Then the next thing we knew, Jon was peering down the back of Tim's shirt for some unknown reason.

"What's down here?" asked Leo, trying to get a look.

"Nothing," Jon replied, then he began looking down the back of Leo's shirt.

"What *are* you doing, Jon?" asked Kirsty, rolling her eyes at Mum.

"Looking for my touch. I thought I'd lost it for a minute there."

It took us a few seconds to catch on, but when we did, we laughed more than ever.

"Nope, you've definitely not lost your touch, old son!" Terry declared.

Chapter 10

O n Saturday afternoon I went back down to the café with Jaimini and told her the incredible truth about Jon and Kirsty. She gasped when I said they were married, and laughed like mad when I told her about how Jon and I had entertained the others with our frog song. We then decided to talk to Jan straight away, because the MS evening seemed somehow even more important now.

"Can Luce talk to you about the MS evening if I help Leah for a while?" said Jaimini, which naturally went down very well with Jan. She even came and sat down at my table with me. Together we worked out the date and the time, then we planned how to advertise the evening. Jan suggested that I got Miss Wickham (I must stop calling her Mrs Olive Stone) to give a talk at our school, and I thought that was a fantastic idea.

It was agreed that Jan would entrust the bran tub, the raffle and the organization of all the acts to us Café Club girls, and that we would show Jan the programme when it was settled.

The others turned up shortly afterwards and we got down to work, organizing precisely who should do what and what it would cost.

When I got home later I was full of our new venture, and my enthusiasm rubbed off on to Mum, too. She said she would make a big cake for people to guess the weight of, she'd make another cake for the raffle, and she'd also get in touch with Jan and take over the catering side of things so that Jan didn't have to worry about all that. I knew why Mum was doing all this: she was very fond of Kirsty, and she was very happy with the way everything had turned out.

The evening was going brilliantly. Everyone had worked very hard to have everything perfect. Mum was right in the centre with Jan. The two of them get on really well together because they are both so dynamic. In a way they were the best double act of the evening.

It was after the first couple of acts, which were Leah on her violin, followed by Fen doing a brilliant jazz dance, that I had looked round at everyone and thought how well it was all going.

Jon, Kirsty and Terry were sitting together,

all laughing and joking. Miss Wickham and Jaimini were running the show and introducing each act. There were loads of kids from our school there, as well as people coming and going, as there wasn't enough room for everyone to stay all the time. In fact, in the end, Jan had made the event into an "all-day jamboree", as she called it. The six of us had worked that day and so had Kevin, Mark and Becky. We'd been operating shifts, which had been very successful. Mark, Becky and Kevin had gone by the evening, and so had most of the food, but Jan had defrosted more and more things to spin it out for as long as poss- ible. We'd sold more than five hundred raffle tickets, and we'd all agreed that this was the best fundraising event that the café had ever held.

"And now for the Kid Conjurors!" announced Miss Wickham in a voice that surprised me.

"She's been drinking, I reckon," Andy said to me out of the side of her mouth. "She's not usually this loud and jolly."

There was a burst of cheering and clapping as Ned, Leo and Tim went to the front and stood on the little stage that we'd erected from blocks borrowed from the twins' primary school. I'd for- given Ned. It wasn't his fault that Chris had been surrounded by his so-called friends when he'd given him my note and my message. For the next ten minutes the three boys did a totally cool act.

I didn't think the twins had it in them, but they were very impressive. Every one of the tricks they did involved all three boys and they worked so fast that the audience was left gasping and clapping. At the end they all bowed, which they'd obviously pre-planned. They looked so sweet and funny, bowing like that. I had to smile.

The smile pretty soon froze on my face because the café door opened and in came Luke, Deep Voice and the other members of the nasty year-eleven gang. Immediately I felt myself tensing up.

"Just ignore them," said Andy, sensing my reaction.

"I can't. It's me in a minute. I'm going to tell Jaimini and Miss Wickham not to announce my act until that lot have gone."

"Look, here's Chris," said Tash, smiling at me, thinking I'd be happy to see him. He'd come in just after the others but he wasn't sitting with them. He'd gone to sit with Ned and the twins. There were a few other people from school there that I didn't really know, but they seemed nice, and there were a few other grown-ups there, too. It was a great atmosphere, apart from those year elevens. I was on the point of telling Jaimini not to announce me when Miss Wickham stood up and my heart sank as I heard the words "olive stone".

"And now for the act that we've all been waiting for," she said, in her totally over-the-top voice. "This is the greatest olive-stone flicker in the West. And I should know, I've been on the receiving end." The whole place laughed. "She also does an interesting double tackle on your handbag, if anyone would like to try her out." The place errupted. "So will you please put your hands together for Miss Lucy Edmunson!"

Everyone cheered and I stood up, but my heart was beating wildly because I was so scared. I'd heard of stage fright, but I'd never realized how bad it could be. I don't know if it was because I was tense, but as I crossed over to the stage at the front, I knocked into one of the tables and sent a cheese baguette flying. I lunged forwards to try and grab it, but finished up flat on my face. As I got to my feet, red-faced and mortified, I realized that everyone was laughing, and I saw Jon give me a thumbs-up sign from the back. Kirsty clapped high above her head. *They like me*, I thought. *They thought that was all part of it!* I looked round and saw that I was right. The whole café wouldn't stop laughing, and I just had to stand there and wait as they clapped and clapped. I couldn't help having a quick look over to where Luke and the others were sitting, and, surprise, surprise, even *they* were clapping.

"What's this?" said a voice from the back,

above the laughter. Everyone turned to see Jon on his chair doing some kind of weird wriggling movement with his body. The laughter subsided and from Jon's mouth came a peculiar gurgling noise. I knew instantly what he was doing.

"A drain laughing," I answered him, and once again the place erupted. This was easy. "OK, what's this?" I yelled out, and I pulled my face into that of a toad and stuck my tongue out, then drew it back in instantly, as though I was catching a fly.

"A frog!" yelled out Ned, which was close enough.

This time, when I glanced at Luke and his mates, they were laughing just as hysterically as everyone else. In fact, Luke had tears running down his face. I didn't know what had made me do the frog face. I hadn't planned it. It was just the effect that Jon had on me.

"Frog went a-courtin', and he did ride, a-hum!" Jon suddenly started singing at the top of his voice, from his chair at the back. His timing was perfect, but then it would be, wouldn't it? He was a professional.

"Frog went a-courtin', and he did ride, a-hum," I joined in with Jon, in my loudest singing voice.

Then Jon jumped down from his chair, dashed to the front, leapt on to the platform with me, and the two of us proceeded to do our ridiculous version of the rest of the song with all the crazy over-the-top actions, while the audience wept with laughter.

"Bravo!" yelled Deep Voice, leaping to his feet when we'd finished.

"Bravo!" cried Luke, following suit.

They were both grinning at Jon and me and clapping their hands towards us. It was a wonderful feeling, receiving all the applause. Jon did a very silly curtsey to acknowledge the audience's reaction, so I stuck my heels together, bent my knees, put on my frog face, and did an even sillier bow, which made someone call out: "Three cheers for Lucy!"

I couldn't work out who it was who'd spoken, but I spotted him on the third "hip hip". It was Chris. He winked at me. Then there were another three cheers for Jon, and during this I clearly heard one of the girls from our school ask Leah who the man was with me.

"It's Luce's brother, Jon," Leah replied.

"Jon who?"

"Jon Baxter," I called out, as Jon and I left the stage, the clapping still going on.

"I thought it was Jon Baxter," Luke said to me as I passed him. "I saw him acting in this play we went to see for GCSE English last year. He played the part of the hero. He was excellent."

I couldn't help smiling to myself. Here was Luke practically idolizing my brother, who'd played the part of a hero, and now Jon was playing that part again, only this time he was *my* hero. How the tables had turned.

Loads of people were patting Jon and me on the back as we made our way back to Kirsty. Then someone stopped me. It was Chris.

"No girlfriend tonight?" I asked him – a bit flirtatiously, I must admit.

"No. Dumped her," he replied, in the same sort of matter-of-fact voice that he'd used when he'd told me he was going out with her in the first place.

"Oh, sorry," I said, because I didn't know what else to say.

"She's not too pleased," he went on, "but then she never did have a sense of humour!"

I laughed and started to head on towards Kirsty. "What's the attraction back there?" Chris asked, grabbing my arm. "Come and sit with me for a bit and tell me how you manage to contort your face like that."

"Tell you what?" I asked him, feeling gobsmacked because the great Chris Harvey had at long last noticed me, and all because he admired my frog face. I decided I *would* sit down with him, partly because my knees were doing that melting thing again.

"I didn't know you had a sister," Chris then said.

I was about to say that I hadn't, when I noticed that he was looking at Kirsty. A lovely feeling came over me, because I was realizing that now I *did* have a sister!

"It's obvious that you're sisters. You look so much alike," Chris said.

I looked over at Kirsty then, and just as though she knew I was looking at her, her eyes met mine and she gave me a very special smile. A sisterly smile.

Join the Café Club!

Would you and your friends like to know more about Fen, Tash, Leah, Andy, Jaimini and Luce?

We have produced a special bookmark for you to use in your Café Club books. To get yours free, together with a special newsletter about Fen and her friends, their creator, author Ann Bryant, and advance information about what's coming next in the series, write (enclosing a self-addressed label, please) to:

The Café Club
c/o the Publicity department
Scholastic Children's Books
Commonwealth House
1–19 New Oxford Street
London WC1A 1NU

We look forward to hearing from you!

HIPPO ANIMAL

Have you ever longed for a puppy to love, or a horse of your own? Have you ever wondered what it would be like to make friends with a wild animal? If so, then you're sure to fall in love with these fantastic titles from Hippo Animal!

Thunderfoot
Deborah van der Beek
When Mel finds the enormous, neglected horse Thunderfoot, she doesn't know it will change her life for ever…

Vanilla Fudge
Deborah van der Beek
When Lizzie and Hannah fall in love with the same dog, neither of them will give up without a fight…

A Foxcub Named Freedom
Brenda Jobling
An injured vixen nudges her young son away from her. She can sense danger and cares nothing for herself – only for her son's freedom…

Goose on the Run
Brenda Jobling

It's an unusual pet – an injured Canada goose.
But soon Josh can't imagine being without him.
And the goose won't let *anyone* take him away
from Josh. . .

Pirate the Seal
Brenda Jobling

Ryan's always been lonely – but then he meets
Pirate and at last he has a real friend...

Animal Rescue
Bette Paul

Can Tessa help save the badgers of Delves Wood
from destruction?

Take Six Puppies
Bette Paul

Anna knows she shouldn't get attached to the
six new puppies at the Millington Farm Dog
Sanctuary, but surely it can't hurt to get just a
little bit fond of them...

HIPPO GHOST

Secrets from the past. . . Danger in the present. . . Hippo Ghost brings you the spookiest of tales. . .

Summer Visitors
Emma thinks she's in for a really boring summer, until she meets the Carstairs family on the beach. But there's something very *strange* about her new friends. . .
Carol Barton

Ghostly Music
Beth loves her piano lessons. So why have they started to make her *ill*. . .?
Richard Brown

A Patchwork of Ghosts
Who is the evil-looking ghost tormenting Lizzie, and why does he want to hurt her. . .?
Angela Bull

The Ghosts who Waited
Everything's changed since Rosy and her family moved house. Why has everyone suddenly turned against her. . .?
Dennis Hamley

The Railway Phantoms

Rachel has visions. She dreams of two children in strange, disintegrating clothes. And it seems as if they are trying to contact her...
Dennis Hamley

The Haunting of Gull Cottage

Unless Kezzie and James can find what really happened in Gull Cottage that terrible night many years ago, the haunting may never stop...
Tessa Krailing

The Hidden Tomb

Can Kate unlock the mystery of the curse on Middleton Hall, before it destroys the Mason family...?
Jenny Oldfield

The House at the End of Ferry Road

The house at the end of Ferry Road has just been built. So it can't be haunted, can it...?
Martin Oliver

Beware! This House is Haunted
This House is Haunted Too!

Jessica doesn't believe in ghosts. So who *is* writing the strange, spooky messages?
Lance Salway

The Children Next Door

Laura longs to make friends with the children next door. But they're not quite what they seem...
Jean Ure

Midnight Dancer

Elizabeth Lindsay

Ride into adventure with Mory and her pony,
Midnight Dancer